ADVANCE PRAISE FOR ROBIN TROY AND
FLOATING

"Robin Troy writes like a bloodhound on the trail of that most elusive of literary quarries: the truth. Superbly written and, more importantly, superbly imagined, this novel is suffused with an emotional wisdom that belies its author's age. Despite the ethereality of its title, *FLOATING* is solid as a rock."
    —Dale Peck, author of *Now It's Time to Say Good-bye*

"I want my MTV—and another book by Robin Troy! Her writing is as spare and hot as the desert that surrounds Ruby and the other gems who populate this enviable debut."
    —Suzanne Strempek Shea, author of *Hoopi Shoopi Donna*

"The spark and deft phrasing that mark a true writer's voice are here in abundance. Robin Troy is the real article."
    —Natalie Kusz, author of *Road Song*

"In *FLOATING,* Robin Troy looks at many kinds of love—maternal, fraternal, erotic—and shows us how tangled and knotted the relationships within one small family can be."
    —Larry Watson, author of *White Crosses*

float-
ing

robin troy

New York London Toronto Sydney Tokyo Singapore

An *Original* Publication of MTV Books/Pocket Books

MUSIC TELEVISION®   POCKET BOOKS

POCKET BOOKS, a division of Simon & Schuster Inc.
1230 Avenue of the Americas, New York, NY 10020

ISBN: 0-671-02449-3

First MTV Books/Pocket Books trade paperback printing October 1998

10 9 8 7 6 5 4 3 2 1

POCKET and colophon are registered trademarks of Simon & Schuster Inc.

Printed in the U.S.A.

For my parents
I think I hear a galloping noise . . .

There were eighteen horses in the corral, four lying on their sides looking dead, the rest standing dead still. Only the heat rippling the air above them was moving. From the ridge where Ruby sat in her truck gazing down, the horses looked like plastic figures rooted to the flat ground beneath them. The two wranglers leaning against the corral fence could have been toy figures, too, ones left out in the sun too long, melting at the joints, their arms and necks dripping toward the sand. Neither wrangler was Sean, she knew. He wasn't anywhere to be seen. But if he had been, he'd have been standing up straight, shoulders back, not a bead of sweat falling from his taut jaw to the starched, dry kerchief tied tight around his neck. If Sean had reason to sweat, Ruby knew, he'd be somewhere indoors, in a dark room where no one would see him, cooling down. The wranglers' small office was a few steps beyond the corral where the two men slumped with their arms slung over the fence. From her truck, Ruby eyed its sagging roof and, below it, the flimsy wooden door, always left open in the summer, now conspicuously closed. *He's in there,* she thought to herself. Her fingers stung from clutching the truck door at the window frame, so she lifted them away and rubbed her hands together. She leaned her head out the window to look closer. The door was definitely closed. *Right in there,* she thought, *there he is.*

On the seat beside her, Ruby's powder blue suitcase was hot to the touch from the sun pouring in through the window. Earlier she had burned her palm on its handle when, with a flash of resolve, she had practiced hefting the weight of it quickly toward her. Now she took the orange scarf from the belt loops of her jeans and tied it around the handle. She tried to imagine what it was going to feel like to get out of the truck and go down there, to actually carry the suitcase to Sean. She'd been packing that case for hours, it seemed, though the truth was she'd spent more time pacing between the closet and the bed, cradling the empty suitcase like an egg shell in her hands. Midway through packing, she'd knelt in the cramped space of the bedroom closet, fingertips pressed against the floorboards, to catch her breath. Even now, sitting frozen in her seat, looking down to the motionless horses and the wilting wranglers, she felt a helpless need to slow things down. Like a pulse behind her eyes pounded the knowledge that *right there, right behind that door, there he is.*

Ruby didn't know that this time Sean was sweating, too. He had spent the night sitting in his truck with one hand locked in place over the ignition, wondering where he should go. He couldn't go home to Ruby. It didn't take much to see that he was avoiding the one conversation they both knew was coming. Sean had spent the dawn thrashing first through the barn at the corral and then through the wranglers' office. In the barn, he threw tools off their shelves, buckets off their hooks, kicked feedbags apart until shreds of burlap lay like fallen leaves over the sandy floor. Logic hadn't gotten him into this mess, he'd thought to himself, and it certainly wasn't going to get him out. By the time Sean thrust open the barn door into daylight again, he emerged in his own cloud of dirt. The two wranglers at the fence lifted their heads just long enough to see him storm from the barn to the office and slam shut the door. With hardly a movement beyond raising their eyebrows, they looked to each other, then dropped their eyes again. "Yessir," one said slowly, pausing to lick perspiration from his mustache. "His brother gets out today."

In the office, Sean ripped his knapsack off the nail on the back wall. He reeled around the room, grabbing everything that was his. A pair of boots, a pouch of chew, his ranch-issued khaki poncho, the lucky horseshoe he'd brought with him when he'd come to Whitticker on the first day of August, just over thirty days ago. He was stuffing it all into his bag as Ruby pulled her truck up alongside the dying saguaro at the top of the ridge. He kicked at the table in the center of the office as she turned off the ignition and put her head in her hands. There was sweat in her palms. His heart was beating in his eyes. The door was definitely closed. *He's right in there,* she thought. He dropped the bag and reached for the flask behind the cushion of the couch. She forced her eyes away from the closed door and tilted her head back against the seat. He took a long, burning swig. She crumpled down level with the steering wheel. He collapsed into the cushion. The heat settled on them so heavily it could have had a body of its own, and under its stifling weight both Sean and Ruby held their heads. *Okay, wait,* she said softly to the air. *Just wait,* he pleaded to the ceiling. They thought backward then. They tried to think what to do next.

There is only one road leading out of Whitticker, Arizona, and Ruby Robert Black Pearson was walking down it—past the sign that reads "Population: 641," toward the rest of the world—the afternoon her husband held up the 7-Eleven at the edge of the freeway with an unloaded pistol. The mechanics at the service station next to the 7-Eleven had kept Ruby's truck jacked up toward the ceiling for the past six days, and Ruby was tired of walking. In high school alone she had walked this three-mile stretch of road out of Whitticker more times than she could remember, promising herself each time that she would keep on going, anywhere but back. But now, years later, with a child and a husband and the resignation that she was destined to grow old in the only town she'd ever known, Ruby would just as soon have had a car, any car, to whisk her out to the edge of the freeway and back before the truth hit her, yet again, that at the end of the road she was turning around. She'd had enough of walking.

Ruby walked to the service station that afternoon like a large, lumbering animal whose long, powerful strides appear languorous and slow until you need to outrun them. The crunching of her old boots in the packed-dirt shoulder could have been the clopping of a horse to any tourist passing with his eyes closed. And Ruby would not have disputed the comparison. It was true that everyone in Whitticker was fascinated by her hugeness, her six feet and two inches, her wide hips that, like the flanks of a young horse at a run, were strong and sensual and sometimes hypnotic, not fat. She was tall enough to keep any man sitting while in her presence, but however domineering she might be, no man seated near her wouldn't rather have been sweeping her off her feet. There had never been anyone, in Whitticker, like Ruby.

She talked out loud to herself as she marched deliberately along the shoulder, throwing declarations to the sage and the cacti that all of them were drunks, good-for-nothings, lumps of burden and laziness that she didn't care if she never saw again. She tossed to the brittle clusters the highlights of a conversation she planned to have later with her husband,

Carl, and as she spat down to her mute desert audience that they were bums, spineless cowards, boring, worthless, childish, skinny little boys who couldn't put their feet down for themselves or their family if it meant saving their own lives, years of disdain rose from deep within her to the prickles rising on her skin. It was an exercise that energized her—not that she needed the rehearsal. For one thing, if Carl was half as drunk as he had been last night when she knocked him off their front porch—threatening to bring the empty bottle down hard on his head if he didn't get out of her sight until he could muster some semblance of a man again—he wouldn't realize he was the center of so much attention before he was face down in the dirt for the second night in a row. And even if he wasn't drunk—if he was just there on the porch with their dog Max and a wad of chew—it would scarcely matter how she chose her words, because Carl rarely responded anyway.

So it was simply to pass the time that Ruby practiced as she walked. The road was flat and straight, the only rise and fall coming from the jagged cadence of Ruby's voice. The 7-Eleven and the service station ahead of Ruby scarred the landscape with their slick red roofs and neon signs. She had often wished that these two buildings and their concrete platforms were better dwarfed by the high mountains beyond them, so that they might appear as inconsequential in the sprawling desert as the individual cars that threaded themselves, like colored beads along a string, down the single road out of Whitticker to this glaring, commercial plot. At least the zoning laws had protected the town from any more of *that* kind of building, Ruby thought to herself. At least Whitticker had *that* much going for it. Even if there were posts you shouldn't lean against and steps it would be better to step over, the wooden storefronts along the main street downtown had a charm that the locals no longer really saw but still took pride in, that the tourists—and there was always a stream of tourists—snapped eagerly with their cameras so they could remember the place where they had swigged beer from a bottle next to a real cowboy, albeit one they'd be relieved to leave behind.

Ruby and Carl used to talk about the day when they might leave. In retrospect, Ruby thought their shared enthusiasm for planning ways out of Whitticker as teenagers had probably brought them together in the first place. Or maybe it was just the conviction they shared that if they wanted to leave, they could. Ruby didn't *dislike* Whitticker; twenty-five years later—years after her mother and stepfather had given up on the town themselves and left—Ruby could still recognize the character in the listing buildings, and her own shining place among them. But what bothered her was that within those buildings no one seemed to question what lay beyond the three-mile stretch of road where their small town spilled into the rest of the world.

Carl, on the other hand, had shown some curiosity. He had moved to town with his mother when he was ten, the new fifth grader from out of state. At Eagle Watch Elementary, he was the only friend Ruby had who could talk about the house where he *used* to live, the craggy passes where he *used* to ride his horse, the back alleys in his old town where he *used* to sit on overturned milk crates smoking cigarettes sneaked from his father's pants pocket. Carl had seen where the highway led—if only from a few states away—and his curiosity, unlike Ruby's, stemmed from the places he *had* seen, rather than the places he had not.

In high school, Carl worked pumping gas four afternoons a week at the station in town. Between customers, he chose maps from the rack by the register and spread them out one at a time over the counter, taking in the names of towns from California to Maine, running his finger along winding routes, counting miles by his thumbnail. For Ruby's seventeenth birthday, he wrapped a map of the United States in flowered paper and gave it to her with a card. She took one look at the map's yellowed edges and threw it back at him. She wasn't interested in a freebie Carl could help himself to just because no one else had wanted it. But Carl had picked up the map and unfolded it for her, revealing a maze of red routes he had carefully drawn in, each of them punctuated by gold star stickers showing where he would take Ruby someday. "I want to see all of this with you," the card was inscribed in the same red pen.

But it wasn't the promises that had drawn Ruby to Carl so much as the energy he put into his planning. The fact that his energy was complemented by sharp cheekbones, deep-set eyes, and confidence didn't slow her attraction to him, either. However, there was something else that drew Ruby to Carl.

It was what had kept them together for years, but now, more than likely, was also driving them apart. Ruby could see how people in Whitticker looked at her, how they admired her bright presence in their town. But only from Carl could she hear it. Only Carl was close enough to tell her how he felt. And Carl felt that Ruby could do anything in the world that she wanted. He told her so repeatedly, and she loved him for it. For while it was one thing for Ruby to believe she was strong and capable, it was something entirely different to be told.

The snag, though, was that Carl had grown resentful over time. In the same years Ruby matured into a young woman who believed she was invincible, Carl became more and more dependent on his identity as her other half. While he always pictured them together in the stories he spun about the future, Ruby was quicker to take his confidence in her potential and run with that alone. After high school, Carl went to work in the Western Wear Outfitters' boot department, where he gradually lost his teenage determinations amidst the size and shape of other people's footsteps. But Ruby he was determined not to lose. She gave definition to his life in Whitticker, even if he did resent the freedom she had—a freedom he had in part built in her himself—to do so. She gave him a stake in the town he seemed less and less likely to leave. And so it seemed ridiculous now, as she yelled to the cacti along the road almost a decade later, that Ruby could ever have hailed Carl for his ingenuity and direction.

The back of Ruby's shirt clung to her skin with perspiration generated as much from cursing the vegetation as from walking the three-mile stretch in the suffocating heat. By the time she reached the service station, where she could see the truck was ready for her, she was ready for trouble. She wanted to give someone hell. But even though cars were parked by the repair shop and in front of the 7-Eleven, there wasn't a person anywhere in sight. How strange, Ruby thought. Not only was no one working the gas pump or coming with a drink or a coffee cake through the door of the 7-Eleven, but there was no sound of anyone at all. Ruby's boots on the asphalt made the only noise she could hear. Too aware of herself for her own comfort, she paused just short of her truck. The driver's door was open.

"Hello?" she called to the buildings, the cars, the spaces around them. Her voice broke into the air like a mistake, like something dropped by accident with a bang. "Hello, hello, hello," she called again, with no response.

There was a shuffle behind one of the cars. A small boy poked his face around a wheel, his eyes red and wet with tears. He clung to the tire as if to the leg of a parent, and his shoulders shivered, although in Whitticker, Arizona, in the middle of July, he could hardly have been cold.

Ruby crouched down so as not to scare him away. "Hey," she whispered, inching toward him as she would to extend a crumb of bread to a wild animal. "Hey, little man, tell me what's going on." Ruby had never been one for patience, but she had learned some with her son, Brian, over the past eight years.

The boy opened his mouth to speak, but could only sniffle and heave. "You're okay," Ruby reassured him insistently, until she was almost close enough to wipe his streaky cheeks. He flinched, snot appearing and disappearing in his nostrils each time he breathed, then pulled away again. Ruby backed up as well, though she wanted badly to yank him from behind the tire and shake out the answer to what the hell was going on. All she knew was that the cars hadn't driven there themselves. But there was no evidence of any person for miles who wasn't crouched down hiding, holding his breath.

"Listen," she said, trying to keep a soothing tone. "You're okay. Everything's fine." She wiped her upper lip, aware that she wasn't even convincing herself. "You tell me where your mom went. Did she leave you out here? I bet she told you to wait for her right here. You tell me, did she go in there?"

Ruby pointed to the door of the 7-Eleven just as it flew open, and Carl, pistol waving, pockets bulging, burst outside, red-faced and raging. The glass pane blew out of its frame behind him and shattered in midair from his force, hitting the concrete with shrill, dangerous cracks. Before Ruby could grab hold of the boy, he let loose a piercing scream in pitch with the breaking glass and buried his face as best he could in the hubcap. Ruby watched in disbelief—amazement, really—as Carl stormed toward the open door of her truck, howling like a madman, stumbling like a drunk. In one fluid motion, he leapt into the driver's seat and gunned the engine to a roar, taking hold of the steering wheel as he would the collar of a man he intended to slam up against a wall and bloody. He pitched his body forward as he leaned on the gas, his face inches from the windshield. The tires shrieked against the concrete, dirt spat up from beneath the truck, and an empty bottle Carl threw out the window landed with a crack that echoed the door shattering, the little boy screeching, and Ruby herself screaming and screaming the very condemnations—Bastard, Moron, Son-of-a-Bitch, Bum— that she had practiced on the cacti and the sage all the way out to the end of the road. And Carl—the Loser, Thief, Good-for-Nothing, Pockmarked Six-Toed Lowlife—even had the nerve, Ruby screamed before she collapsed on the pavement, to take off down the road that left Whitticker behind without her. Not more than forty-five seconds, and her world was upside-down. The husband she had left in bed snoring that morning was burning rubber to who knows where. With who knows how much money. With who knows what lunatic train of thought driving him along. Forty-five seconds and he'd disappeared with everything she might ever have had: easy money, a smooth truck, the fundamental components of a family. Sprawled on her belly on the hot concrete, Ruby didn't know which part angered her the most. She didn't know which part, if any, she hadn't expected.

But one thing she knew for sure, there was no way in hell she was walking all the way back home. She picked herself up and headed back toward the 7-Eleven, hardly considering that if there had been a holdup, there must be people still inside. What she was thinking as she stormed across the lot was that she hated her husband, that she hated herself for not leaving first, that, for a second, she even hated her son, who would grow up with his father's features, Carl's nose and Carl's chin. At that moment, she hated every person in her lousy life who had been even indirectly involved in bringing her to this afternoon, this colossal letting-down. If being deserted could be spoken of so mildly. She would have sworn out loud right then never to attach herself to another person for the rest of her life if it could have kept her from feeling this combination of anger and embarrassment ever again. But as she opened the paneless door of the 7-Eleven, the assemblage she found there stole her breath away, and despite her earlier verbosity with the sage and the cacti, she could not find the voice to say one word.

Growing up, Ruby had seen plenty of fights in bars and rodeos and against school lockers, plenty of broken bodies waiting to be hauled off in ambulances, but that hadn't prepared her for what she saw here: a floor, a dirty, gritty floor, strewn with bodies, close to a dozen, on their stomachs in front of her. All of them lying there, not dead, but looking it. She couldn't hear any of them breathing. On the wall behind the register, the clock read quarter past three. On the counter, a cup of coffee stood with an open creamer beside it. Steam swirled up from the coffee. Ruby could hear the clock's dull, steady tick; without it, she might have believed this scene had been suspended in time. She couldn't tell if the people on the floor knew she was there, if they knew she was Ruby, not Carl. What she could see, once she looked closer, was the slightest rise and fall in their shoulders, indicating that each individual was doing just enough to stay alive. It reminded her, yes, keep breathing.

Counting them fast, she knew what struck her as strangest. There were nine people, all but three of them men, stretched out facedown, scattered like pieces of an odd jigsaw puzzle, in place but not interlocking. In the cramped space, despite the pandemonium in which they must have hit the ground, these nine bodies lay untouching. If their outlines were drawn on the floor, there would be nine figures whose lines did not intersect. *Practically impossible,* Ruby thought. Frightening, that in the face of one stumbling drunk with a gun, nine people didn't come together to take his weapon, force him to the ground. Strange, that minutes after he had left they remained fixed to the floor. Ruby stared down at them as if she couldn't be seeing correctly. She felt her knees go weak and her throat go dry. It was hot, too hot, in the store. *Pull yourself together,* Ruby said to herself without moving her lips. "Get up," she rasped to the group of them as her own body dropped heavily to the ground.

Of course, Carl had thought he had it made. Not because of the paper bag stuffed with money on the passenger's seat beside him. Not because he had escaped with Ruby's finely tuned truck. Those were merely things he'd got away with when he went crazy from comprehending at last that he'd been wrong, that really he'd never have it made. Though any man who'd married Ruby would have thought the same. Carl Dixson grew up the handsome boy at Eagle Watch Elementary and then Wood River High, the new kid in the class whom the girls listed first under the husband category of the fortune-telling games they played on sheets of folded paper at recess. He was taller than the other boys, and skinny, but there was something in the way he carried himself, the way he rolled his bony shoulders and kept his lazy eyes at a downward glance, that even girls barely twelve years old knew instinctively—though they might not yet label it as such—was sexy. And given the rest of the pickings among the budding teens in their listless county, he had been, at least on the surface, a natural for pairing with Ruby.

Ruby had become a source of pride to Whitticker over the years, and with his hand in hers by age sixteen, Carl was at his proudest. The town never had much else to show for itself; no one ever did more than break even; no industry ever came to boom; even the good horses were moved up north before they could win any awards for the honor of Whitticker. But it seemed from the very day she was born that Ruby was prized, as her name suggested, like a bright jewel in the palm of a dirty, calloused hand. She had a loud mouth and a toothy grin, and an energy that prompted everyone around her to get off their butts, come to life, and make a bid for a quick flash of her coveted smile in their direction. When Carl felt she was spreading her smile in too many directions, he would step in to alert overzealous fans that, in fact, her real name was nothing as sparkly as "Ruby" at all.

When she made him jealous—which was often in the nine years they'd stuck it out—he liked to spread the word that, in fact, she had been born Lucinne Robert Black Pearson to a mother who, in hopes of raising a well-balanced child, had

counted through the pocket book of baby names at the Su-
perValue checkout and identified "Lucinne" as the name exactly in the middle. When he felt threatened, Carl let it be
known that Ruby's father had been interested only in having
a son, if he was interested in being a father at all, and that
to appease him, her mother had added "Lucinne" to the full
name of the noncommittal bum she would never actually
marry.

But from the moment Lucinne Robert Black Pearson fell
into a doctor's hands in the Yucca Valley emergency room
with a shock of strawberry hair, "Ruby" was all the name
she ever needed. "Lucinne" disappeared from people's lips
as quickly as Robert Black Pearson skipped town, and even
after Ruby and Carl were married, she was never referred
to as "Mrs. Dixson." To anyone who knew her—and everybody knew her—she was "Ruby." To the wishful men of
Whitticker who hoped someday Carl might be out of the
picture, just hearing the name "Ruby" was enough to bring
to mind those wide, strong hips and those round, pale eyes
that didn't exactly have a color, but burned through you
nonetheless with the slightest, swiftest glance.

When they were first together, Carl relished that simply
saying Ruby's name in the Early Bird Diner at sunrise would
trigger the foremen and miners and cowboys hunched over
the front counter into imagining a pair of long, blue-jeaned
legs dancing like cornstalks in the steam rising up from their
coffee. He felt proud, waiting for Ruby to join him on a stool
at Bar 4 after work. He could sit with his back to the door

and see in other men's eyes a flicker of awe that marked her entrance. Though Bar 4 might have had patrons taller than she, Ruby's face rose above the rest, her angular cheekbones and puckered lips seeming to say, *None of you knows exactly what to do with me.* Few married men in Whitticker wore a wedding ring, but Carl never took his off. Until it drove him mad, he savored the knowledge that people across their small county—men and women alike—looked at him as he passed them on the street, as he sat with one hand on Ruby's knee at Bar 4, and saw the one person who had figured out what made Ruby tick.

But Carl would have held up a convenience store piss-drunk long ago if he'd realized any sooner that neither he— nor anyone else, thank God—was ever going to make it near that close to Ruby. He'd have been better off resigning himself to that years ago. Nine years too late, however, careening out of Whitticker with double vision and more cash than he might soon know again, still he couldn't shake her image from his mind.

It was typical, he thought, punching the steering wheel. He had finally left her, and there she was nonetheless, the first clear thought in his head. Of course, he wasn't surprised. For years, Ruby had been the definitive influence in his life. He knew this all too certainly. So it simply made sense that her image should be right there with him as this final episode unfolded. He only wished he could truly believe that he did not love her, that truly he was better off this way, with the money and the truck and the open road before him. And though he wanted to insist until he couldn't see straight sober that he did not need her in his life, no disregard for honesty, however resolute, could keep him from replaying his fondest recollection of her as he raced to put miles between himself and Whitticker. It was the one sure memory Carl held on to of a time when he and Ruby had indeed been skin on skin, somehow less than two people, more like the same person, that close.

It was an afternoon in early September when they both were seventeen. One year to the day since they had declared themselves a couple inside a janitor's closet at Wood River High, and Carl was driving Ruby to a place he knew about and she didn't. His secret, her surprise. September was never cool in Whitticker, but that particular day was August hot. It had been a summer no one could account for, with enough moisture displacing the usual drought to yield an unprecedented outcropping of wildflowers. Clusters of tall stems waving yellow faces colored the coarse, desert ground. Carl could remember their thick, spicy scent drifting through the open windows of the truck. Ruby had brought a pocket camera, and she leaned way out the window, hip bones up against the door, snapping the shutter as the two of them glided by. Carl still remembered what she had been wearing—besides her blue jeans, of course, which she always wore, regardless of the heat. She had on a light blue tank top with skinny straps that reached down to the curve of her breasts. Her long, strawberry-blonde hair was tied back loosely with a coarse string of almost the same color blue, a string that Carl would later undo when he lay down with her in the spare, bleached grass.

"Where're you taking me?" He could still hear her voice yelling against the wind as they sped onto the freeway.

"Dunno," Carl said, teasing her with his sleepy eyes, reaching his hand behind her neck. She twisted around and playfully bit his wrist, then his elbow, his shoulder, the backside of his ear.

"Hey, hey, hey." He shook his head as the truck swerved into the middle of the road, and Ruby laughed into his ear.

"I'm not letting go until I know where we're goin'," she said, taking his lobe into her mouth.

"Then I'm not tellin'," Carl quipped, tilting his head toward her and thinking that even with tangled hair and dirty jeans and the smell of horse in the heat rising from the nape of her neck, Ruby was the most beautiful woman he would ever know.

Inside the boundary line of South Loquila, he turned off the highway onto a dirt road and made Ruby shut her eyes. He drove several bumpy miles flanked by sage, while Ruby threatened repeatedly to peek. "What in hell are you doing to us?" she asked as her torso bounced from side to side.

"Keep 'em closed," he ordered.

They hit a deep rut, and Ruby used the force of it to collapse her body into Carl's ribs and land with her head face-up in his lap.

"Whoa," he shouted, jerking the steering wheel as the

truck lurched to one side. "Watch out." He kept his eyes on the road.

"Watch *what?*" Ruby teased.

Carl looked down to see Ruby staring up at him, her eyes opened as wide and bright as she could make them.

"Hey, no way," he said, pressing on the brakes. "You gotta close 'em."

She shook her head on his lap. "I can't see a thing except your nose and the sky, so unless you're taking me to somewhere they don't have sky, it's not giving too much away."

"Come on," Carl insisted, but then saw she was staring at him bug-eyed. "Jesus," he said, laughing. "At least leave them normal. You're going to pop something if you stay like that."

Ruby blinked for him and turned her head sleepily toward his stomach. By the time he told her to sit up again, he had pulled the truck onto a field that had once served as a town baseball diamond before being abandoned, like so much else in their county, to a tangle of unruly weeds. Here, however, the weeds had sprouted tall yellow flowers that lapped at the hood of his truck. Their stems reached to his door like spindly fingers beckoning him out. Ruby pulled herself through the open window for a closer look. She stood on the very front of the hood with her arms in the air. The flowers stretched clear to the far end of the field, so dense in places that it seemed Ruby should be able to step off the hood and walk across a soft yellow carpet. Carl had been stunned when he'd first stumbled upon this magically decayed field, and he was happy to see Ruby was equally pleased with his find. At the edge of the hood, she balanced on tiptoes, clasped her hands high above her head, and let out a long, high-pitched holler as if from the very bow of a ship in the ocean, she were about to jump in.

In an area that was probably once the outfield, Carl parted some flowers to make a clearing for their blanket. They spent the afternoon inside the stem walls, eating raspberries from their cooler until their lips and fingertips were stained, and sipping beer slowly because they had the time. But what Carl always focused on when he replayed this day in his mind was Ruby, the sun full on her face, asleep with her head on his knee. He had lowered her head onto the blanket once she was breathing heavily, so that he could step away in search of some small purple flowers he'd noticed sparingly mixed among the yellow ones. They grew no higher than his knees, so Carl walked doubled over, picking them one at a time until he had a solid fistful. He knew she would like them. He believed he knew more about her than other people did. Gathering the purple blossoms in a bunch, Carl treasured the notion that on this perfect day he had Ruby where no one else could find her, sleeping with her hair fanned out and the straps of her tank top slipping off her shoulders like smiles, all for him. When his fist was full, he grabbed one large yellow flower and snapped the blossom off with a flick of his fingernail. He placed the orphaned head on the leaves of another weed, then used the long stem to tie a bow around his bouquet.

He sat down on their blanket and lifted her head back onto his knee. He brushed the feathery petals against her eyelids, her cheeks, and the line of her jaw. She had fallen into a heavy sleep, and even as her eyes finally opened, she wasn't fully awake. When she saw the bouquet—and this was the memory Carl most liked to focus on years later—she didn't speak, or take it in her hand right away. Instead, she lingered in her dreamy state, and fixing her eyes on Carl's, she worked open the button of her jeans. She pulled down the zipper, too, and with a series of gentle tugs and wiggles, she slipped them off the rest of the way.

Her underwear, like the shirt she wore, had thin strings on either side. She rested her hands on her hips and pointed inward to the softness between her legs. Carl saw at once why she pointed, why she didn't need to speak. Sprinkled over her white cotton underwear was a pattern of purple flower buds. She ran one of her fingers along the string down to the inside of her thigh. She rubbed her thumb back and forth over the buds, looking up at Carl the whole time as if to say, *See, you know me this well, you've picked the perfect thing.* At least that was how Carl liked to remember it. He liked to remember how she hooked her thumb through the string and slipped the underwear, the little cotton buds, away from her.

She took the flowers from him. She pulled a petal from one of the purple heads and placed it where her underwear had been. She pressed it on her skin so that it would stay. Ruby pulled every petal from Carl's tidy bouquet until they

25

filled the space her underwear had covered minutes before. They wove in and out of her light red hairs as naturally as if they had grown there.

And there was no need to talk about it. Without a word, Carl took off his pants, pushed up her shirt, worked loose the blue string from her hair. Like a mirror, he placed his body over hers and against the purple petals. It was the most perfect memory he had. There was no question for him, then or now, that at that moment they both had believed they were meant to be. But what Carl did not know about Ruby then was that really she believed only in herself. It didn't mean she wouldn't love him or that she wasn't interested in being his wife. But it did mean that she could live without him, that at the start of any day she was prepared to rise on her own two feet, whether he was at her side or not. Even at the most unlikely moments, Ruby could maintain this distance that Carl would never understand. But no matter what he had learned about her over the years, he managed to keep this one memory intact. He ended it every time while they were lying in the grass, before they went back to the truck, before they discovered, six weeks later, she was pregnant.

After that, Carl knew his luck was running out. It made him angry to think back on the sour turns his life had taken, and so, speeding out of Whitticker, he did his best to focus on the good: purple petals, a stack of cash, his truck cruising with a purr. Of course, being dead drunk shed its rose-colored haze over everything, too, and Carl wasn't feeling bad. He thought this time he might make it. In fact, he believed he would. But as the road forked to South Loquila, he saw flashing lights come into his rearview mirror, heard sirens wailing behind him, and from that point on he couldn't remember clearly what happened next.

Three police officers stopped him just inside the boundary of South Loquila. One clamped on the handcuffs; one slapped a red sticker on the truck; the third palmed Carl's head and dunked him into the backseat of his cruiser. And because it was South Loquila where the officers smelled his breath and took his gun, Carl was delivered to their station instead of back to Whitticker. He was shoved into the single holding cell of the South Loquila Police Department, onto a threadbare mattress that lay atop a wooden shelf jutting out from the wall. He sat with his elbows on his knees, cupping his hands around his face like blinders, shutting out all but the sight of his own two feet. He was too drunk to stand steady on them if he tried.

What a ridiculous day, he thought, scowling. All he'd intended when he got out of bed that morning was to go to Bar 4 and settle his sixteen-dollar tab from the night before. His head had ached, but no worse than it ever did on any morning of his day off. And Carl was always good for what he owed, so he arrived at Bar 4 shortly before noon. Joe Meyers, a wrangler Carl had once worked with at the Flying C Ranch, was at the bar.

"Back on our side of the fence today, are you?" Carl

jabbed at Joe, who now worked the L Bar Ranch, thirty miles up the road in Lawrence.

"Straddling it, anyway." Joe said, smiling. "Like always."

Carl took a stool himself. "What brings you here at this hour?" he asked.

"Saddle shopping," Joe answered, extending a hand to Carl. "L Bar needs a half-dozen at least, so we're down for the day. Thought we'd swing in here first to say hello." Joe pushed his stool back so he could introduce the man who'd come with him. "I don't know if you've met Darren."

Carl nodded to a barrel-chested man he did not recognize.

"Darren lives in Lawrence," Joe said. "Darren, this is Carl. We used to give each other hell down at the Flying C."

Carl put out his hand.

"He's Ruby's husband," Joe added.

Carl drew back before Darren could reach him, and took hold of the bar's thick, rounded rim instead. He dug his nails into the mottled, old wood. If just *one* person could leave out that qualification, he grimaced. If for *one* day he could simply be Carl. He felt his cheeks flush with anger. If just *one* person in their goddamned county could get through his own plain-Jane life without knowing Ruby. Without being so goddamned impressed by Ruby. Carl's resentment of her lay right at the surface; it triggered his bad temper quickly.

"Yeah, sure." Darren smiled, his eyes lit up. "I know Ruby."

Carl turned to the bartender. "What do I owe you?" he snapped. "Sixteen?" He reached into his front pocket.

"In fact, I bumped into Ruby, oh, not more than a week ago," Darren continued, his voice chipper.

Carl pulled some balled-up bills out of his pocket, ignoring Darren.

"At that food plaza rest stop off Seventy-six going south to Morraine. She was there in line, getting a soda or something. Said she was on her way to pick up her son. That sound right? She's got a son who takes some kind of lessons down in Marshall? Carl?"

Carl scrambled to count out bills, wondering if he was misunderstanding Darren. He was angry enough now to hear things wrong.

"I don't know," Darren puzzled. "I could be off. But Ruby *does* have a son, doesn't she, Carl?"

Carl crushed the money in his fist and kicked the base of the bar. *"Her* son is *my* son," he spat. *"Our* son. *We* have a son." He couldn't believe he needed to defend the very fact that he was a father. Whether or not he had a good relationship with his wife, *that* was arguable. Whether or not Ruby had always been faithful to him, *that* he had debated before. But clarifying the very fact that Brian was his son? This conversation, he raged, had gone too far.

Carl overturned his stool as he shoved the money back into his pocket and stormed out of Bar 4. He charged across Main Street and up to the Quick-Wick liquor store, where he laid out the sixteen dollars for as large a bottle of whiskey as it would get him. He stormed to his car in a fury he felt sure would get the best of him. Walking out on Ruby might well destroy him, but damn her for leaving him no other choice. Damn her for laying claim to everything in their town, from the attention of strangers to their own child. How on earth, he boiled over, had he let her get away with so much? He had no reason to stay. After all, he was known only as Ruby's husband. Apparently, he wasn't even known as Brian's father. It would matter none if he were gone.

Carl sped home, his throat burning with whiskey, and left the engine running while he ran inside to grab his gun. Thinking about it now, he was shocked that he had had the presence of mind *not* to load it. He took nothing else with him. He would have hightailed it out of town without making any stops at all, except that he had no money. He hadn't exactly prepared himself for this day. In fact, the rest of it he remembered only vaguely as he sat, head in hands, in the holding cell in South Loquila. Ruby's truck had been outside the repair shop, freshly detailed and tuned, when he'd pulled in to the 7-Eleven. That had been an unexpected stroke of luck. Carl had parked his own temperamental pickup around back, then explained to the repair man in the lot that he needed the keys to retrieve his wife's truck. He explained, as they both stepped into the store, that he was doing her a favor.

"Mr. Dixson." Carl heard someone saying his name, but he kept his eyes on his boots. "Mr. Dixson," the officer began again, louder this time.

Carl raised his head. The officer stood with his chest out,

thumb hooked over the holster on his hip. "First off," he said, "you should know your wife has been contacted—"

"Don't talk about my wife," Carl grumbled. He didn't need to hear any more about Ruby.

"You should know that she's been contacted and that—"

"I don't want to fucking hear it," he shouted this time, pounding the mattress and grimacing at the puff of dust that rose up.

The trooper swaggered closer to the cell and took two bars in his fists. Carl read his badge: Officer Harrison Landell. "What I am going to *tell* you," Landell continued, "is that—"

"Fuck my wife!" Carl yelled, slapping both hands hard against the plaster wall.

Landell crossed his arms over his chest and paused, letting silence set in. "Well, okay, Carl," he mocked calmly. "But do you always give permission, or doesn't Ruby generally make those decisions for herself?"

Carl lunged at the bars, roaring with a jealousy so potent that Landell took two fast steps back. On the third step, he turned toward his desk and added coolly over his shoulder, "She said don't bother calling. She said waste your phone call on someone else."

Carl hit the wall with his open hand and fell back on the shelf. *As if* he were going to call Ruby. He had been leaving her, for God's sake, at least for a while. He'd had money in his pocket. He'd had drive, even if it was fueled with non-

sense. Of course he wouldn't call Ruby. She could do whatever she wanted now, for all he cared, as if she ever hadn't.

He started thinking back to what followed their afternoon
in the field, to how big her belly had grown, to how much
Brian had cried, to how she'd shifted her attention away from
Carl to everyone else in Whitticker before her belly was even
flat again. He stopped himself there.

On one wall of the cell, a pink elephant was painted from
floor to ceiling, huge and bright and sickening. Carl lay down
and stared at it, wondering what the hell it was doing in
there, what pediatric office waiting room wall it had wandered from. It wore a gold crown on its head and a string
of pearls around its neck. Its eyes were painted purple. Carl
realized how drunk he was then, how likely it was that the
glaring elephant might be just enough to make him throw
up. It was cruel, he thought, for someone to have painted it
there. What prisoner would want to look at something so
foolish? Who the hell had painted it? He felt himself growing
hot with anger. The worst part of it was—and, at this, Carl
even felt sober for a moment—it reminded him of being
young. It reminded him that he'd had twenty-five years to
make a life less foolish than this, that he had failed, that this
was failure.

If Carl could have asked for anything as he tried to fall
asleep on the wooden shelf that night, it would have been
for someone to tell him that it wasn't all his fault. He would
have felt better hearing that since the beginning of his relationship with Ruby, he'd never really had a fighting chance.

Because if there was one flaw Ruby had, it was that she had grown too tall and been raised too high ever to be paired with anyone else. So even if Carl thought he had struck gold with their wedding eight years earlier, he'd actually been destined to look small from that day on, to suffer by comparison. The bottles he kept open and the silences he fell into stood as evidence of that. What Carl should have realized nine years ago was that the point had never been for Ruby to find an equal, for her to find her match. He should have realized that two people of Ruby's character could never share a space so small as Whitticker. It could only be left to the imagination, what would happen if two such people ever tried.

If there'd been someone there to tell him these things, Carl might have fallen asleep with an easier mind that night. He might have decided, in the morning, against calling his brother, Sean.

Sean was asleep on a blanket in front of his trailer in Windpoint, New Mexico, when his phone rang, and he got up stiffly, cursing the heat, the hour, the ring. He ducked his head to step through the door, but banged it anyway on the frame.

"Goddammit," he snarled, grabbing his hairline and rubbing his palm back and forth over his forehead. He was already seething when he picked up the phone. "Unless you're Mr. Goddamn Wintertime calling to tell me this bullshit heat is gonna let up in my lifetime, I'm not gonna take it lightly that you got me up at . . . at . . ."—he squinted across the kitchenette to check the clock—"my God, at six fucking twenty. Hello?"

"Sean, hi," Carl spoke softly into the phone. Jail or no jail, he had always caved under the force of his younger brother. Jail or no jail, it had always been humiliating.

"Carl? Well, my God. Three months later, and all of a sudden you can't even wait till noon? What the hell—"

"Yeah, well, they don't let you make so many decisions for yourself around here," Carl snapped. "Listen, Sean, I'm in jail. In South Loquila. I've got maybe five, maybe ten minutes, and I need your help. Think you can sober up long enough to hear me out?"

"Fuck you, I'm not drunk." Sean kicked at a cabinet below him, and its door swung open.

Carl ignored him. "Have you found another job yet?" he asked.

"Three months later and you care?"

Carl closed his eyes. "Have you?"

Sean leaned one hand on the counter. "Not that it's your business, but I've got a few things lined—"

"So you don't yet. Good. I mean, listen. I—"

"Wait a second, Carl. What the hell did you do?"

"It's not import—" he started, and then, in the interest of time, changed his mind. "Drank a bottle of whiskey and visited a convenience store. Just that I had a gun. Not loaded. I'm thinking no more than eight, ten months and some probation. But, Sean, shut up. The point is, right now I'm up to my neck in shit. I'm stuck in here for a while anyway, and I need a favor. Jesus, I'm swallowing my pride so hard here I'm gonna shit it out before I finish. But there's one thing I need, Sean, that no one else can do for me, if you'll hear me out." Carl stopped for breath, and Sean said nothing.

"Sean?" he said. "Will you hear me out? What do you think?"

There was a pause on the other end while Sean ran his hand over his face and held on to his chin. "I think I haven't seen you in five years, Carl," he said. He lowered the phone to his thigh and gazed out the door toward his blanket. He counted to ten and tried to guess what Carl could want. They both thought Sean might hang up.

"And five years ago it had been ten years since we lived under the same roof." Sean spoke again. "And even longer since we'd acted like a family, and drunk or sober, crack-of-fucking-dawn or not, I'm not about to right off say yes— three months after you wouldn't call me back when I was looking for a job—to some favor you need because you got yourself thrown in jail. I'm not dumb enough to feel sorry for you just because you got yourself in a shitload of trouble. I've been out of work for five months here, Carl. So, no thank you, big brother. However I might be able to help you out, I'm not interested." Sean nodded his head and put his free hand down the front of his pants.

Carl had expected nothing different. It was a stupid move to have called him. One more fumble to chalk up for Carl, one more smack in the face from Sean. The way it had always been, whether they were under the same roof or not. Carl remembered something he'd forgotten until then: he had not cried when their father had taken his belongings and Sean out of their house to who knows where on that hot July afternoon when Carl was ten. He had stood in the hard dirt of their front yard and watched placidly as his father made a few, quick trips between the house and his truck, carrying two duffel bags, their red cooler, several cardboard boxes with the flaps hanging open at the top. While Sean had climbed into the truck, Carl had straightened out the tangled dog chain in the dirt and walked back and forth along the top of it like a tightrope. He stepped heel to toe along the dusty chain and thought what a relief it would be to have them gone. No more of their parents' yelling. No more of his younger brother's taunting. Now he would never have to endure another of his father's disappointed stares that made him feel he would always be the lesser son.

Not until years later did Carl realize that other families did not split up the way his had. It never occurred to him, standing in the dirt that day, that most kids' parents did not announce over dinner one night that they were dividing themselves. He would be a teenager before he comprehended how heartless their decision had been. At ten years old, as the truck pulled away, he smiled that the bunk bed was his alone. And only when he pushed the chain into a pile again, once they were out of sight, did the sound of its clanking metal make his home seem quiet and his stomach turn queasy. After that day, Carl and his mother had stayed in the house only a few more weeks themselves before they moved to her sister's place in Whitticker, where all the girls judged Carl the handsomest boy in town because they would never see him next to Sean. From then on, Sean kept moving with his dad to small, rough towns where he learned early on he would never have to worry about comparison.

In the station, under fluorescent lights, Carl felt a wave of nausea come over him. "I'm sorry, Sean." He began again. "It's just that this is a bad situation, and I need one small thing from you so it doesn't get any worse. My God." An officer nearby cleared his throat and pointed to his watch. "And, Sean, I don't have much time."

"Carl, if you even think I'd—"

"Sean, please." Carl's grip on the phone had become so slippery that the receiver fell out of his hand, and he scrambled to retrieve it.

"There's no way in hell—"

"Can't you at least hear me out?" he pleaded, recovering his hold.

"Don't you have a family?" Sean retorted, and Carl was suddenly short of breath.

"What?" he faltered, as if he'd somehow been caught in a lie.

"I mean, you've got a wife and kid, and you get one phone call, and you choose to call a brother you wish you never had, who hasn't thought twice about you—"

"My God, Sean." Carl's voice was strained. "I mean, my God. There are just some things better left un—"

"What's her name, again? Your wife?"

Carl turned away from the officer, facing the wall. "My

wife's name is Ruby, Sean. Ruby." And with her name on his lips again, he knew the game was up. He leaned his forehead against the wall and stared down at his boots. He'd hardly slept at all last night because of her, and the little that he had dozed, she'd been there in his dreams. He almost forgot about Sean on the other end of the line, angry as hell at six-thirty A.M. He thought again about how he could still love the woman who had driven his life into the toilet, and himself into jail.

"But she's hardly my wife anymore," he mumbled. "This is what I'm trying to get at, if you'll listen. Do you remember Evelyn?" Carl managed a smile as he said her name. The police officer in the room raised his head.

Evelyn was the horse their parents had given them when they were boys. They'd watched her birth fifteen years ago at the corral where their father worked as a wrangler, and their mother had let them bring the filly home on the condition that she could choose the name. When their father left home with Sean, Carl took care of Evelyn by himself. She became his closest companion. He occupied his early mornings feeding her under a silver sky. In the afternoons, he groomed her in their makeshift stable, telling her stories about school until his mother came home from work. When they moved to his aunt's house in Whitticker, where there was no stable at home, Carl explained to Evelyn that she would be sharing a bigger stable with other horses, and he boarded her at the Flying C down the road.

The wranglers at the Flying C grew accustomed to seeing

Carl first thing every morning. They were amused by the wiry, serious kid who brought his own backpack of horse brushes and treats each day and kept to himself while he cared for his horse. They teased him that with this kind of devotion, he would make a good husband someday. By the time Carl was a wrangler himself at the Flying C, everyone swore he and Evelyn shared their own language. Evelyn was a finicky horse, and far from the most desirable, but she behaved for Carl under any circumstance, and he defended her vehemently to the other wranglers. She was one of the few constants Carl had in his life, and he took comfort from knowing that she was his alone. Even behind bars in South Loquila, Carl was heartened to single her out as the one facet of his life he had never compromised for Ruby. He had dedicated himself to spending time with Evelyn every day, and he felt certain that she was the one thing about which Ruby—as unlikely as it might seem—had grown jealous. Ruby mocked him for spending so much time alone with his second-rate animal. She nagged him about when she could ride Evelyn. Not that Ruby actually cared if she ever swung her leg over the animal's back or not. But Ruby did seem to care, Carl thought, about the way Evelyn had always divided his attention.

"Well, either she *is* your wife or she *isn't,*" Sean said abruptly, thinking over what Carl had said about Ruby. He spoke as if Evelyn had long ago stopped registering in his mind.

"Will you listen?" Carl's voice was impatient.

Sean held the receiver at arm's length from his mouth and groaned. "Hurry up."

"Okay, good," Carl said. He started talking fast. "See, the thing is, I was in the middle of leaving Ruby when all this happened. But that's something I don't have time to get—"

"You wouldn't have been gone for dinner," Sean cut in.

"Sean, shut up," Carl snapped. He raised his voice almost to a shout, and the police officer moved a step closer. "You have no idea," Carl said, shaking a finger in the air. "I had the truck, I had the money—for the first time . . . No, no, I'm not going to get into this. The point is, Ruby has had enough things her way, and I can't . . . I'm *not* gonna take it anymore."

Carl looked down to the line of scarlet half-moons he had raised on his forearms clenching himself the night before. Jail was bad enough. But the prospect of Ruby completely free now, with him unable to keep any track of her at all, unable at least to be in their home, where her scent would be on the sheets, was unbearable. It didn't have to make sense that he loved her. It didn't matter that it was probably too late to keep her from having her way.

"The point is, Sean," Carl said, unrolling his sleeves over his forearms, "the point is that now Ruby has the house, she has the truck, she has my son—"

"Yeah, what's his name again?" Sean interrupted.

"Brian!" Carl hissed, exasperated. "He's eight years old. Now, keep your mouth shut. What I'm trying to say here is that with me gone, Ruby's gonna get everything she wants—

I mean, more now than ever—and I've already had enough of that. And there's only one thing she's always wanted that I've managed to keep my own, and that's Evelyn. Evelyn's *mine*. Everybody knows that. Ruby hasn't once been on her, and she bugs me all the time about when I'm gonna let her have that horse, which is never. I will *never* let her have that horse. So that's why I'm calling, Sean. That's my favor. I need you to come get Evelyn for me, cart her out of town before Ruby takes her, too, and then we'll have one thing kept safe in this family." Carl collapsed against the wall and noticed how tense his shoulders had become.

Sean didn't say anything right away. He was counting again in his head. "Isn't Evelyn about ready for the factory by now?" he asked, needing more than ten fingers to add up her years.

"Yeah. Yeah, she really is," Carl said sadly, "but see, there's a part I didn't get to yet. The part I didn't get to is she's pregnant. I thought it might be too late for her, but I bred her anyway with this quarter horse down at the Flying C. I want to keep her going, you know? So she's done really well—better than anybody thought—and now she's got a month or so to go, and I need you to be there when that foal comes out. Ruby's gonna take her otherwise, and I'm telling you that can't happen. That *will* not happen, Sean." Carl could feel the back of his collar damp with perspiration. "So what do you say?" he said. "You're still looking for a job. What's a few months in Whitticker? My house has room, you've got no reason to turn down what'll probably be a

43

prizewinning horse, and Ruby can't stop you if you say I want you to have her. So I need to know, Sean." Carl raised his eyebrows in anticipation.

Sean cleared his throat as if to say something, but then stopped. The line went so quiet Carl thought it might have gone dead, and he held the receiver out to check it. Sean's laugh came shooting out of the receiver and hit Carl like spit between his eyes.

"Sean?" Carl called, pressing the phone back to his ear.

"This is fucking ridiculous," Sean said, still laughing, though the truth was he had already started thinking about Carl's request.

Carl clamped one hand over his forehead and closed his eyes. It was as he might have expected. "I shouldn't have called," he said, wondering how he could ever have thought this might work. He was ready to hang up.

"I mean, I just don't know." Sean kept going as if Carl had pressed him. "I don't know who you think you are, Carl, but all I can say is this is a fucking lot for six-thirty A.M., and all I can say to you right now is that either I might think about seeing to this little favor of yours—because this place is a hellhole I could use a break from anyway—or I might not, but—"

"As long as you've got your options straight," Carl said dryly, and he hung up the phone. With his hand dragging down on the phone cord, he puffed his cheeks up with air, then blew it out as a sigh. In the station with the officer listening, he was too disconsolate to have noticed the quick shift in Sean's attitude. It didn't register with him that Sean had moved from a "No way in hell" to a "We'll see" in a matter of moments. All Carl knew hanging up the phone was Sean wasn't coming, he himself was going to jail, and Ruby would be on her own now, as she wanted.

But in Windpoint, New Mexico, just after sunrise, Sean was having different thoughts. It hadn't clicked when Carl first explained it, the whole picture of this favor. Sean hadn't remembered, right away, her name. But now he did recall the first time he had heard it, standing in the hallway of Carl's house as he had been leaving five years ago.

That visit to Carl's had been a mistake. Sean had been driving home to New Mexico after a rodeo in Preston, Arizona—one that hadn't been much fun. On his way to the rodeo two days earlier, he had seen the exit sign for Whitticker along the highway, and the sight of it had made him pause. He knew his mother and Carl had moved there ten years earlier, and it bothered him to pass so nearby without stopping. All weekend, as he combed the rodeo grounds, he looked into the booths and crowded stands as if he might see Carl. He wondered if he would recognize his brother, and the question dampened his mood. Sean couldn't shed the sensation that his family's past was catching up with him. He spent both days at the rodeo bothered by the prospect of passing the sign again on the way back home.

Sean turned off in Whitticker that Sunday because his head was too cloudy to think clearly about the consequences.

If he were completely honest with himself, the truth was he had always been fighting the impulse to find Carl again. And so, as he approached the Whitticker exit, tired and hung over from the weekend, it actually seemed easier to turn off than to ignore the hole inside him that had been created by the loss of his brother.

Carl had been easy to find. The first person Sean asked on the main street of Whitticker told him all that he needed to know: his mother had left town two years ago with a wrangler twelve years her junior, but Carl had settled into his own house with his wife and their child. *His wife and their child,* Sean repeated as he followed the directions to Carl's house. Had enough time passed for Carl to have his own family? Sean lay one hand flat on the steering wheel and slowly tapped his fingers against it. Nine, he counted. He and his father had lived in nine towns in the past ten years. Three states, nine towns, twelve different apartments or houses or converted motels that he could remember. In one town in southern Nevada, they had lived so many different places, Sean had driven home to the wrong address on more than one occasion. Once, after a night of drinking, he got so far as trying to jam the key in an apartment door before he realized he no longer lived there.

At Carl's house, the front door was ajar. Sean parked his truck at the end of the driveway and opened his door just wide enough to slip out. His feet touched down in the dirt like an anchor. For ten years, he had been moving faster than he could pack his bags. For the past two days, he'd been drinking and gambling, unaware of the time. He'd awoken on a motel room floor that morning and spent all of five minutes pulling up his pants and wetting his hair before he'd climbed into his truck. He'd driven dangerously fast across the state with only a cup of coffee inside him, not stopping except for gas, and to ask the man in Whitticker for directions. But gazing down the short driveway to Carl's house, Sean had come to a halt. His brother's front porch appeared impossibly far away. Each step he took toward it seemed slower than the one before, and by the time he had reached the porch— by the time he stood dazed in front of Carl's open front door—the careless whirlwind of his life came to a hideous, grinding standstill.

It reminded Sean of witnessing, as a child, an eighteen-wheeler lose control down a narrow mountain pass. He had watched the truck veer off the road onto a runaway ramp of chunky gravel layered deep as a grave. The wheels had lashed into the rocks with a monstrous noise, and then its whole towering body had shuddered to an eerie, irreversible halt. When Sean finally knocked on Carl's door, when Carl came around the side of the house from the backyard, when the two of them stood motionless, staring at each other for the first time as adults, the silence, Sean would never forget, had been no less staggering.

Sean knew at once he had made a mistake. He cursed himself for not anticipating what might come of his visit, though he couldn't have foreseen his emotions had he tried. He moved back down the porch steps as Carl walked around front. They stood a few feet apart in the dirt yard. Staring at his older brother, Sean was struck by how much he and Carl did, indeed, look like family. He studied Carl's shoulders, broad as his own, and felt furious for their similarity. In their likeness, he saw for the first time how much he had missed. From the instant Carl appeared, Sean was blindsided by the enormity of what had been taken from him before he'd been old enough to understand. He knew it didn't make sense to direct his anger at Carl, but he was on the verge of shouting when his brother spoke instead.

"I can't *believe* you came here," Carl sneered with disgust. His eyes were narrowed, incredulous. His voice was low but barely restrained.

Sean nodded imperceptibly, squinting in discomfort. "I can't either," he said, almost inaudibly.

Carl snorted in contempt and kicked his toe in the dirt.

Sean bowed his head against his brother's disapproval. "Jesus, I don't know—" he muttered into his chest.

But what Sean did not know as he faced Carl was how certainly his brother had come to believe, over the years, that he'd been abandoned by his father and Sean, rather than that their family had decided to split. Carl couldn't help but feel he was the boy who had been left behind while Sean and his father packed up their pickup to go off into the world and share their lives as men. Sean didn't know how Carl's bitterness toward them had festered, how incensed Carl was by Sean's nerve to appear on his doorstep, on a whim, and disrupt the life he had been building on his own.

"Well, let's not just stand here," Carl said flatly, gesturing toward the door. He stepped past Sean, who didn't move. From the porch, Carl glared down at him. "Come on," he said, reluctantly waving him in. "Let's go inside."

In Carl's kitchen, Sean said no to everything. No, he didn't want a drink. No, he didn't want to sit. No, he didn't need any water. No, regardless of the fact that he hadn't eaten all day, he wasn't hungry. Sean heard how difficult he sounded, but he couldn't calm the tension brewing inside him. All he wanted was to get on the road and gun the truck back to his life in New Mexico, where he need never confront this mess again.

"You know, I should really go," he said abruptly to Carl after a perfunctory tour around the house.

Carl was standing in the backyard, and Sean was still at the top of the cement steps outside the kitchen's screen door.

"What?" Carl snapped. He craned his neck forward as if he'd misunderstood. "What?" he said again.

"I've seen enough," Sean said, though he didn't mean to sound rude. He meant to say this visit was more than he could stomach, but he chose the wrong words.

Carl's temper boiled over. "First you show up here?" he hissed, his eyes fixed on Sean. "You decide to waltz in here like you can do as you damn well please?" He was raising his voice. "You can just say screw whatever anyone else might be trying to do with their life, I think today I'll go ahead and turn someone's life upside down because I feel like it? Is that the kind of person you're all proud to've grown into, Sean? Is that it?" Carl held his hands out in front of him, waiting for an answer.

Sean fixed his eyes on the ground and told himself not to respond. There were three empty beer bottles on the step beside him, and he concentrated on them, on their brown glass, as he tried to shut out Carl's voice.

"And now after you've gotten whatever you want out of this—I don't know, you've seen whatever miserable glimpse of my life you hoped to find here—now you're ready to disappear again, no big deal, just take off back to wherever it is you are now, where no one expects you to stick around anyway?" Carl was shouting. "Is that it? Because if that's it, Sean, then you're something else. If that's it, then you can go on and get out of here now. Get out of here before my wife comes home with my son." Carl was trembling as he yelled. Ten years might have passed, but he had never stood up to his brother this way before.

Sean started to turn away. He didn't have the patience—and maybe not the strength—to explain his behavior.

"I have a family now," Carl screamed. He wasn't going to let Sean leave before he'd finished what he had to say.

Sean wheezed through his nose, struggling to hold his tongue.

"Get that?" Carl kept yelling. "I don't need this shit anymore."

Sean gripped the railing and clenched his teeth, but Carl wasn't finished.

"So you can take your thirty-minute peek at my life and

get the hell out of here and know that I don't care where you take it as long as you don't come back."

With that, Sean raised his leg behind him and kicked the empty bottles into the air. They flew in three separate directions, and one shattered on a rock in the dirt. Carl shielded his face with one arm as Sean turned and headed back inside. He stormed through the kitchen, knocking a chair over backwards as he went. By the time he reached the narrow hall to the front entrance, Sean had too much fury pent up inside him to saunter casually out the door. He had done his best not to lash out at Carl's tirade, but *he* had always been the controlling brother, not Carl, and leaving without fighting back was not his style.

The hallway was dim except for a narrow rod of afternoon light slanting in from the open front door. Sean tilted the face of his watch into it so he could see how long it had been. The watch read five-fifteen, just thirty minutes since he'd arrived. Ten years, thirty minutes, Sean considered. If he hadn't pulled off down that road to Whitticker, those thirty minutes would be no different from any others in the long period of time he'd spent apart from his brother.

Sean knew his anger at Carl that afternoon was neither entirely warranted nor especially well-defined. But he also felt certain Carl would agree—had they been able to discuss it—that shouting and kicking empty bottles were simply ways of venting the frustration left over from the broken childhood neither of them had asked for. Besides being angry at Carl, though, Sean was unnerved that he felt irritated at himself as well. As much as he wanted to justify his own position, Sean had to admit that because it was ten years since he'd last seen Carl, maybe he should have called to say he'd be driving through. Maybe there was something he should have done differently. A wave of doubt swept beneath his skin, spreading red blotches from his neck through his cheeks right up to his hairline. It was a foreign feeling to Sean, and the sense it implied of losing control compelled him to reassert his authority before he walked out the door.

In the hall, he spread his legs apart with his ankles pressed against either wall. He dropped his chin to his chest and raised his hands above his head. After three long breaths, he clenched his fingers into fists and began pounding them back and forth against the wood-paneled walls. He started slowly at first, then faster. When his hands began to hurt, he kicked at one of the walls, then at the banister, then at the wall he hadn't kicked first. His movements came automatically, a punch at this, a tear at that, a series of kicks anywhere in between to give his sore hands a break. It was the kind of rage that reminded Sean, no matter how old he was, he had not outgrown the effects of his family's disintegration. It was the kind of rage he depended on to diffuse his anger without letting anyone see what bothered him. So it felt like a natural progression to him, having bowed his head and swung his limbs to exhaustion, to catch his breath, undo his belt, and tear open the line of buttons down his jeans.

He held himself out toward the hallway wall with one hand, arching his back. His other hand gripped behind his neck. Before he let loose—maybe to swing his pee in a rude, sweeping S over Carl's wall—he paused to feel himself with a gentleness incongruous to the moment. He tightened his grip on the back of his neck and let his mouth slacken, his eyes fall closed. Only with his eyes closed did Sean become aware of other sensations around him, the muffled sound of a boot rocking over the worn wood floor, the scent of a body that wasn't his own, that carried the taste of something singularly feminine through the air.

Sean opened his eyes to see a woman standing inside the open front door. The shaft of light cut across her, highlighting half of her large figure in the low sun, leaving the other half dark. Sean could see one eye, one long leg, one half of a beckoning, paralyzing smirk. He could see one half of a head of hair that looked to have been set on fire. For no more than an instant, though it seemed like much longer, he stood there and she stood there, neither of them speaking. Sean felt himself grow inside the palm that still kept its grip, but he was less humiliated than he was sure that the eye he couldn't see was staring into his as intently as the one he could.

He pushed himself back inside his jeans while she watched. He fumbled with his shirt and tugged at his belt, and she just stood there. In the silence between them, his movements were magnified, made louder and cruder than they actually were. He straightened his shirt over his shoulders, then put his hand down his pants again to readjust, but she didn't move from the door. Sean was sweating, and she was taking it in with an unrelenting stare. She was letting him know that he was caught. But he wouldn't have admitted to feeling awkward at that moment, because there was something less obvious to it than that. With his pants down, dick out, he was surely less embarrassed—his ego oddly less damaged—than he should have been. The shaft of light railroaded his vision to the one half of the woman alone, and as sure as she was stunning, he was stunned.

"Ruby," Carl's voice called suddenly from behind the house, breaking the spell between them. It was the first time Sean had heard her name. She turned swiftly and walked back out the door around the side of the house. Sean moved directly after her and out to his truck, the late light of day finally revealing a flush of embarrassment in his cheeks. Part of him was following her as he rushed outside, part of him running away.

Five years later, he still didn't know which it really had been. But either way, it had been too compromising an incident for him. It was a moment that Sean had never been able to shake. He wasn't accustomed to being caught with his pants down, hands red, being anything other than smooth. A dozen years of growing up alone with a father who believed a pool cue, a deck of cards, and a bottle of beer were the staples of any worthwhile education, and Sean had naturally become a slick enough manipulator to get whatever he wanted. And all he'd ever consistently wanted was enough money for one solid horse, a string of flimsy women, and the kind of respect you got with a little bit of awe and a healthy dose of fear. At six foot five, with broad shoulders and skin golden as the desert sand at sunset, Sean had more than all of that. Twenty-three years old, and he had a stash of rodeo prize money, a list of women behind him longer than he cared to count, and hands so deft no man wanted him in his bar after dark with those tools he'd been so expertly raised on: that pool cue, that deck of cards, any bottle of beer. They were tools he could find in any town where he chose to settle a while, which suited Sean well because he didn't ever take much with him when he moved.

Sean was good at leaving things behind. Growing up with his father, he'd learned to make it look easy from an early age. A blue banana-seat bike he'd bought with his own money from a pawnshop in Mason, Arizona; a trampoline in Canyon Home, New Mexico, that his father had given him as a late birthday present after he'd won some money in a bet; even a horse, once, that his father felt was too lame to make the trip out of the last town where they'd lived in New Mexico. Anything that didn't fit easily into the back of a pickup didn't make the trips with them.

Sean would always remember one night when he was fifteen and his father made them pack and leave especially fast. They'd been living in a mining town a few miles inside the northwestern corner of Arizona, and his father had been crossing into Nevada most nights to gamble. On this one night, he'd gotten into some kind of trouble he never explained to Sean, and he'd broken down their door, reeling drunk in the middle of the night, shouting that they had to be gone before morning. Sean could still hear his father's words.

"If we don't get on the road now," his father said, leaning into the kitchen counter, "things are gonna get sticky."

Sean had been sitting on a stool at the counter, eating noodles out of a plastic container, when his father burst in. There was one dim light above Sean's head.

"We're gonna get on the road," his father slurred, "and we're gonna go until we find someplace open, someplace we've never been before, and then we're gonna sit down there and have some coffee and some breakfast, and we're gonna talk about this then." He'd lifted a bundle of money out of his coat pocket and almost lost his balance. "Everything's gonna be fine," he'd said. "I, for one, am going to have eggs and toast, and everything's gonna be fine." He'd teetered at the counter, thumbing through the cash, and seemed to lose his train of thought.

"We're only *not* going to be fine," his father had continued, pointing the money insistently at Sean, "if we dick around here worrying about what we need and what we don't need." Sean remembered how his father's eyes had looked uneven on his face, one half-shut, the other alarmingly wide open. "That's the way you get stuck to things," he'd said. He'd spoken with such disdain, as if there were no worse fate than to be a grown man with some kind of attachment in his life.

In retrospect, it saddened Sean to remember how he had taken his father's words as a lesson. He sometimes wondered, once he was living on his own, how his life might be different if he hadn't been raised by a man who had loyalties to no one, who thought, God forbid his son should grow up to drag the foundation of a life around with him like a piece of toilet paper stuck to his heel.

But Sean had, more or less, grown up his father's son. He had moved to a handful of towns by himself in the few years since he and his father had parted ways. He'd been living in Windpoint for a almost a year and a half when he'd lost his job as a horse and cattle wrangler, and had resorted to calling Carl. Not that he had cared about losing his job. It was time to move on anyway; a year and a half in any place was at least a half a year too long. Sean liked small towns best because they were simple to blow into and shake up. But the drawback, he found, was that their resources ran out fast, and Sean got restless when people's reverence for him became old hat. He liked to keep things fresh. And so, sitting in his mobile home with an ex-girlfriend's wilting spider plant and a bottle of beer whose label was peeling off in the heat, Sean conceded that after five months of wondering if and when another wrangling job might come along, the possibility of doing Carl a favor was actually starting to sound attractive.

But what stirred Sean even more was the picture of Ruby's outline, which kept appearing to him since Carl called. Sean had never been able to shake the recollection, and he'd spent more time thinking about it than made him comfortable. It was a nagging reminder that someone out there to whom he had no claim had already gotten the best of him. So after two weeks of thinking—and of making sure Carl would be long gone by the time he arrived—Sean packed his bags. He loaded his truck, hooked the empty horse trailer to the back, and without so much as locking his front door or saying a good-bye to anyone, he turned over his engine and left Windpoint in a spiral of dust. He drove to Whitticker in a single stretch that would have worn out any other driver, but as he approached the one road leading into town, Sean was by no means thinking about rest. He was just getting warmed up, by the time he pulled in, to dig his heels into the dirt of his next small town.

Nobody was home at Carl and Ruby's when he arrived. Sean got out of his truck quietly and stood in front of their modest wood-shingled house. Before he moved any closer, he reminded himself that this time his brother had invited him here. This time, in fact, Carl had begged him to come. The house was as Sean remembered it: beige, weathered, a buckled porch in front that they might have done better without. The middle second-story window had only one shutter, and above it a row of loose shingles drooped limply over the roof toward the gutter. The front yard was all dirt, and lying in it was a dog with a streaky brown coat who jumped up and growled as Sean approached. Sean stepped gingerly onto the porch and peered in the window. He could see nobody inside. He stepped back down to the dirt and walked around the house, looking in windows. Still, he found no one on the property. Sean considered that Ruby might have moved away after Carl left, but he could see too many things inside. Back in front of the house, he put his hands on his hips and felt his shirt wet just above his belt. He could have sworn that it was even hotter in Whitticker than in Windpoint—an impression that, true or not, seemed better than the possibility that he might be nervous. He wasn't sure, when he took a deep breath and figured he had to give it a try, that this wasn't going to be a mistake.

"Ruby?" he called into the wide-open air. He bit the inside of his cheek and waited for that long leg, that sharp eye, to appear. "Ruby?" he tried again a little louder when they didn't. Despite all of his past thinking about her, it was the first time he had spoken her name. And then, as if to remind himself that she wasn't the only person he'd been expecting to find, he added, hollowly, "Brian? Are you here?"

But for the time being, taking a seat on the uneven top step of the porch, Sean was left alone.

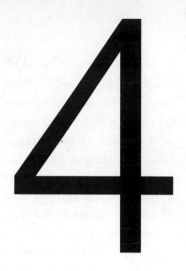

B rian let the water move him where it would. It pushed at him from underneath, nudging his bottom, his shoulders, the base of his skull. He let it carry him like a sturdy, steady animal whose broad back dipped and swelled to the movement of four wide paws. Sometimes he arched his neck, raised his chin, and let the water reach up just over his hairline. Sometimes he swept his arms from his sides to his ears and felt the water run soft like flour through his fingers. All over his body, it felt cool and soothing and far removed from the harsh, dry desert just outside. He kept his eyes closed and felt the weight of wetness on his lashes. Sometimes he pretended they were stuck. He let the water fill his ears, and it filled his head with a hum that helped him lose his bearings. He liked to imagine—though he'd never flown—that the hum was the roar of a plane's engines at takeoff, and with the water rocking him, lifting him, taking him away, he was gone. He was gone far from the cracked dirt, the burning asphalt, the dried-up plants—the only earth he had ever known. He was drifting to a world polarized from his own. The water covered all but his nose and his lips and the tips of his toes, and as if on air itself, he was floating.

There was nothing Brian liked more than this. Pruned skin, blue lips, he would have endured them forever if it meant he wouldn't be made to get out at the end of the second hour. Four times a week, fifteen minutes each time, this was what Brian looked forward to most. The last fifteen minutes was the relaxation period that their teacher, Sherley Wadlow, saved for floating.

Sixteen other boys and girls, aged eight to ten years old, were in Brian's class at the Y. The were the Middie group, one step up from Peewee, and Brian was the youngest. Other eight-year-olds had been held back in Peewee at the end of the prior spring season, but Brian had risen all the way to the top of the ten-year-olds. With the skinniest legs, the tiniest suit, Brian would stand on the racing blocks with an intense, furrowed brow that made the older boys and girls snicker until he had beaten them all, once again, to the other end of the pool.

Out of the water he was timid. He didn't talk to the other

children much, though they mostly liked him. Rather, Brian absorbed his surroundings with darting eyes that never stopped finding something to be fascinated by. When he did venture to talk to another swimmer, it was inevitably to ask questions—*How long do you think a person could hold his breath under water if he had to? Have you ever sat Indian style on the bottom of the deep end? Do you think you will grow up to look more like your mother or your father?* Brian was the most inquisitive eight-year-old Sherley Wadlow had ever taught, and she often told him so on the afternoons he convinced her to let him stay late, to float in the diving area while the older group, the Sharks, gathered at the shallow end. On such occasions, Sherley would linger at the locker room door with Ruby, talking casually about Brian's rapid progress. The first time she'd met Ruby, when Brian had begun his lessons three years earlier, Sherley Wadlow had hardly been able to speak, she was so surprised to see her. Brian overheard her telling another instructor how shocked she was to find that the mother of her fastest, smartest swimmer was none other than Ruby Pearson.

Really, it made no sense. They weren't even offensive to Ruby, the jokes people made about whose son Brian was. He followed in few, if any, of his parents' footsteps. Brian was miraculously towheaded, though no one else in Ruby's or Carl's families ever had been. At Eagle Watch Elementary, where Ruby and Carl had begun their long struggle toward high school graduation, Brian was winning his teachers' praises and bringing home words like "amorphous" and "autonomous" on flash cards. In his free time, he never went near the horses Carl and Ruby had raised and ridden all their lives. Instead, by the age of five, he'd begun practicing laps of absurdly short length in an aboveground pool at a schoolmate's house just down the road. When Brian first asked Ruby if he could take swim lessons at the Y in Marshall, a larger town forty miles south, she'd decided for sure that there had been a mix-up. She imagined her true son many miles away on horseback, a cigarette tucked into the dark hair behind his ears, a forged note in his pocket excusing him from school. That was the son she could relate to.

Nevertheless, Brian had persuaded her to give in. After months of his begging, Ruby agreed to take him four afternoons a week, plus two Saturdays a month for meets, all the way to Marshall and back so he could swim on the Peewees' team. Three of those afternoons, she drove him straight from her morning shift at the Whitticker Inn Trading Post, where she'd sold Native American crafts since high school. If the afternoon girl arrived punctually at one o'clock, Ruby had just enough time to drive Brian to his lesson, never more than a few minutes late. Sometimes she watched the swimmers warm up before she ran errands in Marshall. And when she returned to the Y at pickup time, Ruby often gazed at Brian in the Olympic-size pool, in his tiny racing suit that made him look gangly and small, and wondered how his floating body had actually come from hers.

On the afternoon that Sean pulled into town, Ruby was running late to pick up Brian. With the Sharks already gathering, Brian was in the pool enjoying extra floating time. He was spread out under the diving board, eyes closed, letting the water take him where it would. He had drifted far away by then, well into the hum that never failed to carry him off. And on that afternoon, as had been the case at every recent lesson, he wanted to escape his real life more than ever. He wanted to get away from those components of his life that had fallen apart in the past two weeks: his mother, his father, the general notions he'd held of what it was to be a member of a family.

Even at a young age, Brian had never fooled himself that he was part of a normal family, though he hung on to the belief that if one of the three of them got hurt or sick—or certainly if one of them disappeared—the other two would care. But when Carl had been arrested, Ruby hadn't even asked the police how long she might be husbandless. Brian never saw or heard her shed a tear. For the past fourteen days, he had been trying to understand how none of what had happened to his family felt sad to anyone but him. Newspaper reports made it sound like excitement. Downtown, it became the speculative talk he overheard as drinkers headed into Bar 4. But at his own home, it was merely the reason that the toilet seats weren't left up anymore, that the TV wasn't always on. There was still beer in the refrigerator now, two hours after it was purchased.

Brian felt like screaming. At night, he would sometimes

open his mouth wide into his pillow. But like his submissive father, he never made a sound. Instead he lay awake on his back, arms spread out to his sides, waiting for a dream to take him far away, as if the sheets beneath him were water. While he waited, he kept replaying the same recent events in his head. And as no dream had yet proved good enough to sweep him away, some version of those events continued to seep into his consciousness when, weary from thinking, he finally fell asleep. Even floating in the pool that afternoon when Ruby was late, Brian was fighting to chase away one such image.

In his mind, it stayed stubbornly fresh. He was angry that even in the water, now, he had to struggle to push it away. He dipped his head underwater and shook his hair, but the scene was still in front of him. He and Ruby were standing in the brightly lit jailhouse in South Loquila the day they had gone to say good-bye to his father before Carl was transferred to a prison in the far corner of the state. Carl was standing before them with his fists at his sides, a guard positioned inches away. It was so awkward, all of them standing in the spare office, waiting for the county van to arrive. Any minute his father would be taken away, and Brian was wondering when they would be together again. *I might be twelve by then,* he was thinking. *I might be a teenager. Old.*

The dirt on the station's linoleum floor grated loudly each time one of them shuffled his feet. No one said a word. Carl looked at the floor. Ruby looked over her shoulder as if she were bored. Brian twisted his watch around and around on his wrist and checked it each time the face came up to see how much time the three of them had left together.

He wanted to reach out and touch his father. His eight-year-old mind was convinced the guard would handcuff him, too, or toss him in jail if he did, but he longed to touch his father's hands, his father's shoulders. He was afraid he might forget them if he didn't. Brian urged his muscles to move forward, toward his father, but his skinny limbs locked in place. There might as well have been a wall between him and Carl. Brian couldn't move forward one inch. He heard the van's wheels grinding on the gravel driveway as it pulled in, and yet the only movement he could make was a frightened, involuntary flinch.

Ruby never budged either, although Brian was certain that if she wanted to, she could. He didn't believe she was actually going to carry on like this right up until Carl was gone. She hadn't spoken to Carl, hadn't visited, and Brian hadn't once heard her inquire what would happen to her husband. Brian stopped looking at his watch and eyed her intently, waiting for the second when he was certain she would move.

The sound of crunching gravel caused everyone to jerk their heads toward the door. Soon two more guards swaggered in talking loudly, but they, too, paused the instant they crossed the threshold. They stopped mid-step, as if something infectious in the room's air enveloped them and froze them in place. They waited by the door until the other guard motioned for them to take Carl by his arms. Brian saw their nods and turned desperately back to Ruby. She was staring at Carl directly now, and his eyes were fixed on hers. Brian felt sure that she would do something. He knew his mother couldn't be as cold as her expression, and he felt his heart race in anticipation of the affection he could hardly wait to see.

What followed then seemed to happen in slow motion. The guards took Carl by his elbows and guided him forward. Reluctantly, he took his first step toward Ruby and Brian and the door. Brian swiveled toward Ruby, incredulous that she remained standing there blankly. *Please,* Brian begged in his head. He curled his toes in his shoes. Carl came forward and brushed his hand over Brian's hair. He closed his fingers over his son's head, and Brian felt the pressure and the heat of his father's hand. Then Carl stepped over to Ruby and stopped.

The tension between them filled the room. Brian saw all but the space around Carl and Ruby go suddenly dark, as if he might be blacking out. Carl opened his mouth, but if he said anything, Brian didn't hear it. The hum was too loud in his ears. He gaped at his parents with his heart splitting. *Come on,* he mouthed, without making a sound. Ruby glared at Carl with hard, cold eyes. *Kiss him,* Brian pleaded in his head. He was sure that he must be screaming. *One kiss,* he begged. It was all he wanted to see. He craned his neck forward to make Ruby do the same. *Please kiss him,* he pleaded again. He clutched his spindly legs and imagined how it would look: his mother leaning over to kiss his father, one tender kiss on his lips, and then it would be okay that they wouldn't be together for a while, because they would both remember that they were in love. They had to be in love. It was all that Brian wanted right then, the reassurance that this one detail, at least, was as it should be.

The guards gave Carl a final prod, and he leaned forward. "Ruby," he whispered into the nape of her neck, a forlorn sound that hardly left his lips. Brian held his breath. But Ruby did not even meet her husband's eyes. She jerked her head away from his breath, and the guards directed Carl out the door. The whack of the screen door made Brian jump. His father was gone. His mother hadn't kissed his father. His mother didn't care. These images would run through Brian's head for a long time on. He felt the pressure on his head as if his father's hand had never left. He didn't remember the car ride home. He didn't remember the ice cream cone Ruby bought him. What he remembered was that she'd said nothing, that his father had said his mother's name and she had said nothing back. It would go around and around in his head.

"Brian." Someone was calling his name. "Brian, come on," he heard indistinctly, aware that with his ears filled with water he could make her try harder. He floated on his back and let her nagging voice remind him where he was. He was in the pool in Marshall with the Sharks waiting by the steps. He didn't feel like answering. It was his mother's voice, why should he? This was a new attitude for Brian, trying his best to disobey his mother. In truth, it was an attitude he was having a hard time playing out. But after all, she hadn't answered Carl. So in the past two weeks he had worked hard to ignore his bedtime, keep conversations short, pick discontentedly at his dinners. Some days he was more successful than others, but generally his efforts were thwarted by the fact that he was eight years old and Ruby was not only his mother now, but his entire family.

"Brian, I mean it," she shouted again down at the pool. He had floated near the side, and she had her hands on her hips towering over him. "Get your butt up here by the count of ten, or you're gonna be walking it all the way back home. I know you can hear me."

But Brian pointed his toes to the wall and pushed off toward the center of the pool.

"One," Ruby shouted. "Two."

On three, Brian flipped over onto his stomach, kicked his legs in the air, and plunged down toward the bottom. He let the air out of his lungs and hung motionless in the water before he was all the way down. *Like a coin in a paperweight,* he thought, *suspended.* He loved to feel his body completely immersed in fluid. Even if for only a few seconds, he loved to experience being wholly connected to something else. Like air, but with a substance more like a body, the water never allowed any space between itself and his skin, and that constancy comforted him. Brian loved thrashing his arms and legs around and keeping the water always right there with him. How wonderful, he thought: no matter what, to stick together.

Above the surface, Ruby was fuming. She knew Sherley Wadlow and the Sharks were watching, and she knew she looked foolish shouting at the water. Brian, too, knew how angry his mother would be, and he didn't want to go back up. But his air was running out. When he broke the surface, he drew breath quickly, only to hold it again as he met Ruby's eyes. She was standing over him, glaring as he had never seen before. He had finally crossed a line. It made him feel momentarily guilty and sure that he deserved anything she might say. But, to his surprise, Ruby said nothing at all. Brian continued to tread water, expecting her to start in on him, but she never did. Finally he swam to the side and heaved his stomach onto the wet concrete. Then she turned and walked away from him, back outside toward the truck.

Brian took his towel from the bench along the wall and wrapped his shivering body in its folds. He sat down and draped it over his head, so that everything was dark. If he thought his mother might be happy to see him, he would go to her. If he could believe she was upset with his father gone, he would willingly get in her truck. If he thought his father would be at home, he would want to go. But Brian didn't know what to expect when he got home. He listened to his steady breaths fill the miniature shelter he'd made with his towel. A toaster oven, Sherley Wadlow had once called this position. Only so long can you stay inside warming up before you have to pop back out. Already his breath was making the tiny space hot and uncomfortable. But he didn't want to come back out for air just yet. He didn't want to drive back home. Either way, he was burning up, and he felt sure that soon something would explode.

S ean and Ruby both saw it coming along the ridge leading up to Buzzard Peak. Sean was lighting a cigarette
on Ruby's front porch when he caught a quick flash of orange
in the distance. Ruby was driving past the service station
with Brian beside her when she noticed two attendants pointing up at the peak, hands shading their foreheads against the
sun. The distant flicker signaled that a fire had started. Summer was almost complete. Sean held his burning match at
arm's length, blocking the flame on the ridge from his sight.
Ruby craned her neck to keep an eye on the flare as she
continued slowly past the peak toward home.

"Bri," she said softly, nudging him. "Look up there."

Brian didn't look. He'd dropped his chin to his chest as soon as they had left Marshall, and he wasn't going to give in with just a few minutes to go. That much he was learning from Ruby.

"Oh, come on, Brian," she said again, pushing at his shoulder. "There's a fire starting on Hospital Hill. You can just see the littlest bit if you tilt your head." She poked her finger under his chin and tried to lift it. "I know you want to see it," she teased. "I know you're gonna look."

Brian twisted his head away, not looking, and folded his arms across his chest. "It's called Firehouse Hill," he snapped. "You don't even know the name."

Ruby gripped the steering wheel as if she might strangle it. "I don't know why I waste my time," she said, leaning into the pedal as they picked up speed.

They moved fast toward Sean, who was eyeing the flame through the smoke of his cigarette. Hospital Hill, Firehouse Hill, he didn't know the difference, only that in August, in a dry, desert town, a fire was a fire. They came and went like any good county rodeo that stayed a few days, keeping everyone on the edge of their seats, hopefully blowing out of town before anybody got hurt, but always leaving some degree of destruction in their wake. The fire Sean sighted was on the rocky hill below Buzzard Peak that did, in fact, go by two different names. When Ruby and Carl were in high school, it was called Hospital Hill for the kids who cruised their four by fours up and down its treacherous incline too fast, too late at night, and generally with too much beer inside them. But after a boy three years behind them had been killed careening over a boulder and the police had cracked down, Hospital Hill was renamed Firehouse Hill for its other distinction. Toward the end of nearly every third summer, it caught fire.

The name was a way of separating the old from the young. Ruby and Carl were old. Brian was annoyed that they couldn't get it right. For him it had always been Firehouse Hill that he watched each summer for a flame. The hill extended off Buzzard Mountain, which stood at the outskirts of Whitticker as the only distinctive landmark in any direction. Though a mountain of notable size, its peak was unexpectedly flat and truncated, stunted to a round, dull nub that would never realize its potential. The mountain lurked beyond Whitticker as a monument to the town's residents who suffered from a similar affliction. And with its relative height and expanse of scrub, Firehouse Hill off Buzzard Mountain was vulnerable when the air grew too hot, the ground too dry, and a bolt of lightning struck. It was where Brian always looked for fire.

But in the car with Ruby, he wasn't going to let her think that this summer was just like any other, that he was as excited to look for flames this year as he had been in the past. Secretly, though, he was reassured by the fire's return. It made him remember the last blaze three years ago, when he and his parents had been shut inside their house together for two days.

The smoke had been thick enough that year for the county to issue a warning, and most stores had closed while television and radio reports urged everyone to stay inside. Ruby and Carl and Brian had shut all the windows in the house and stripped down in the heat. Carl wandered around the kitchen in his underwear, restlessly opening and shutting cupboards, while Brian stared out the window in his Peewee racing suit, sizing up the smoke. Ruby wrapped ice cubes in dish towels, and the three of them stood idly, rubbing the sacks along their necks and foreheads. The ice cubes' muted chatter filled the kitchen until Ruby broke the monotony.

"A picnic!" Brian remembered her announcing, as if she'd made a discovery.

Carl had scowled at her at first for suggesting they go outdoors, but she'd ignored him and jogged to the refrigerator on the balls of her bare feet.

"Who says you have to have a picnic outside?" She'd smiled at Brian, patting his Peewee suit. She'd slapped slices of bread on the counter in pairs, end to end like open books, slathering every other one with peanut butter. "You guys have a better idea?" she'd challenged.

Carl had shrugged his shoulders and smiled in surrender. It was rare that all three of them were home together in the middle of the day. "No, ma'am," he'd conceded, opening cupboards one by one.

Brian remembered racing down the basement stairs for their cooler, and feeling the temperature drop as if he were plunging into deep water. The chill of the basement's concrete walls had been a relief, but Brian hadn't lingered. He'd heaved the cooler into the kitchen, and within half an hour of Ruby's proposal they had it packed full, a batch of sugar cookies on a sheet in the oven. The kitchen was unbearably hot from the cooking, and Brian and Carl carried the cooler into the living room, where Ruby had cleared out the furniture and laid a blanket in the center of the room. She'd drawn the curtains against the smoke and lit a candle on top of the television to honor the fire. On the floor beside them, she plugged in their radio and tuned it to a station playing twangy country ballads. The three of them sat in the dim room eating peanut butter sandwiches and potato chips and plums that spilled juice over their chins. Ruby brought the mixing bowl from the kitchen, too, and Brian ran his fingers along the inside, scooping up the leftover cookie dough. He washed down the grainy clumps with gulps of fruit punch and wished for the smoke not to lift in another day. He watched as his mother and father took sips from the same beer bottle and sang to each other lyrics of the radio's familiar songs, and he developed this snapshot of his family that he would keep close from that day forward.

But driving past the ridge with Ruby now, Brian kept his head down to show her that this year he didn't care if a fire came or not. He let out a dramatic sigh to prove it.

"I don't give a damn either, Brian," Ruby said immediately, narrowing her eyes, "whether you see the stupid fire or not."

She rolled her window down the rest of the way to get more air. She pointed her nose into the wind to see if she could pick up the scent of burning yet. When she reached their driveway, she pulled in fast, and when she slammed on the brakes, a shield of dust flew up in front of her. When it settled, there was Sean. He was sitting on the porch, elbows on his knees, knees spread way apart. His second cigarette hung between his fingers, fingers between his legs, a thin line of smoke rising up against his body like a line of chalk, dividing him unevenly.

Ruby sat forward in her seat, curious. She felt an extra surge of blood run through her at this unexpected turn in her day. "Well, look what we've got here," she said, cutting the engine. "Looks like someone's found his way—"

"Dad?" Brian cried out, opening his eyes. He lurched toward the windshield, squinting to clear his blurry vision.

"Hell, no," Ruby said as she swung her legs out the door.

Sean watched her legs slide, one, two, from behind the door to the ground, the first complete picture of her he'd ever seen. When she ran one hand from the top of her butt down the side of her thigh, Sean took it in like a draw from his cigarette. For that second, it filled him.

There were no more than fifty feet between them. It was enough distance to hide the color of his eyes and the dirt under his nails, but not nearly enough to keep Ruby from recognizing that this was a stranger, someone new in town. She could see the contour of his broad shoulders and the color of his skin, browned from the sun. *From working with the horses in the sun,* she decided, glimpsing his horse trailer. On the surface, there was nothing he was missing.

She looked from his trailer to his license plate and noted that he was far from home. As she started toward him, she didn't question why it was *her* doorstep he had come to. He was new, was all she was thinking, and it had been a while since she'd used her charm on a man she didn't already know. She pushed her shoulders back and put on the smile that had worked for her many times before, the one that might as well have been a mask, except that it was comfortable. Always in these situations, she was comfortable. The only difference now was that she wasn't in a bar or on horseback or facing a crowd. This time the man had come to her house, and it looked as if he'd been waiting for her. This time, Carl was far from Whitticker.

Ruby pointed to his license plate and laughed out loud. "This isn't the 'Land of Enchantment,' Cowboy, if that's what you're looking for," she called to him, all big smile, all big teeth. She was just starting up. "There's a couple turns you missed."

Sean nodded and realized he'd never imagined how her voice might sound. It sprang out brash and hard, surprising him. He ground his cigarette on the step below him and moved his tongue along the inside of his cheeks for saliva. "Yeah," he said, kicking the butt away. "Sometimes I get turned around."

"That what you call it when you miss a whole state?" she

asked, taking a few calculated steps toward him. His eyes, dark brown, came into her view.

Sean laughed and sat up straight, shifting his hands to rest on his thighs. It would be best, he decided, to follow her lead.

"Like today you just got up all muddled, maybe salted your coffee and had two creams with your eggs"—Ruby picked up speed—"and then all of a sudden your lefts and rights went out the window and the next thing you know you're looking for New Mexico in the middle of Arizona, and, bang, just like that, here you are, in who-knows-where to you, straightening it all out on my front porch?"

Sean peered over his shoulder at the front door and then down to the wooden boards where he sat as if he, too, were surprised to find himself there.

"Something like that," he said, squinting past her, locating the orange flicker on the ridge. "Here I am, anyway."

"Any idea where?" She pretended to look around, as if she needed a clue. She had sidled to within a few feet of him.

"The slightest," he said, and lowered his eyes from the hill onto hers. He was having a hard time keeping them still. He had never, in the presence of a woman, felt so little control over where he should look.

There was no way for him to know that Ruby had as much running through her head. She linked up with his eyes for only a split second before she turned and backed off toward her truck. She was shaken by the way this stranger, relaxing on her own front porch as if he'd been there to watch the whole day go by, seemed at least as comfortable as she. Maybe, she thought, even more so. As she backed away, she had the feeling he was someone she might have been supposed to know. If not for the New Mexico plates, she would have believed they had met before, maybe at a county event, maybe downtown, maybe standing at her own doorstep. He seemed somehow to belong there.

Ruby opened Brian's door and made a sweeping gesture to suggest that he get out. "Gonna stay in there till the next time I want to go somewhere?" she asked when he didn't budge. "I have to talk to this man here, Bri," she said, doing her best to make obligation out of curiosity just by saying it was so, like spinning truth out of a lie. "Go on inside," she urged sharply, and pulled him down out of the truck. She swatted his behind, and he jumped away from her hand, hanging his head as he ran past Sean and into the house.

The screen door slammed, then the door of the truck right after it like an echo. Ruby looked at her reflection in the window. She squinted her eyes, studying herself, then started walking back to Sean. It was a walk she had done a million times before in other places, and yet she couldn't account for the sensation that this time it was even more familiar.

"So, Cowboy," she began again when she reached him, a casual, mocking strength in her voice. "Can I get you a beer at the end of your day, or did you get your good sense lost on the way to New Mexico, too?"

Sean raised his eyebrows and regarded her, puzzled. "You really don't know me," he said slowly. It was almost a question. He was perceiving, gradually, that here was a possibility he hadn't anticipated, a twist in the plan that interested him. Low in his stomach, he felt something stir.

"You're not the first no-name stranger I've had a beer with," she said. "Don't flatter yourself."

Sean looked her up and down as if finally seeing her for the first time. By the subtlest shifts of her body, he measured her command. She was his brother's wife, he reminded himself. She didn't know who he was.

"I'm, ah—" he started, not wanting to. He fixed his eyes on her hips and felt regret already setting in. "Actually, I'm not a stranger." He spoke quickly, hoping she might not catch his words.

Ruby was shaking open a kerchief from her back pocket, but she stopped and held it still, caught off guard by his serious tone. She stared at him to see if what he said was true, to see if she could place him.

"I'm actually . . ." he started again.

"Well, of course you're not a *total* stranger," she interrupted quickly, covering her tracks. She was searching her memory to find where his face might have settled long ago. She wiped the kerchief back and forth along her throat longer than she needed to.

"Obviously you're not a stranger," she reiterated, "or you wouldn't be sitting here on my porch so natural that you might as well have already gone inside and helped yourself to a beer." It made so much sense as she said it that she began to feel secretly uneasy. "But see, the thing is," she continued, purposefully louder this time, "whether you're coming or going—and whether you bought me a drink the last time you passed through here or just wanted to—see, the thing is I don't remember you. So to me you're as good as a stranger, and whyever you're here, we're going to have to start from the beginning again. So I'm Ruby," she said, extending her hand, exhaling a trace of relief.

Sean studied her outstretched hand and almost laughed aloud at how vastly he had misjudged this moment. Where he had expected to be cowering before her with promises never to try pissing on her walls again, he was instead taking her hand to rekindle an acquaintance that did not yet exist. She offered him the chance to start over again, far removed from any allegiance to in-laws or brothers or family. It was luck too good to discard right away, and while Sean didn't really intend to take advantage of her mistake, the notion that just once—as in a snip of a dream—he might have the chance to touch her was enough that the whole truth could wait.

"I know," he said, more confident than he had been initially. "But see I never thought of buying you a drink either way. I'm here 'cause I know Carl." He almost disappointed himself by staying so close to the truth.

Ruby withdrew her hand and wished she could suppress the flush rising in her cheeks. She had hit on plenty of Carl's friends before. It was just that this didn't happen to be one of them. This was a friend of Carl's who was here to see Carl, not her, and she'd made the mistake of assuming differently. Nevertheless, it didn't mean something couldn't happen.

She eyed Sean shrewdly, and he thought she might know he hadn't told her everything. Under her scrutiny, he shifted his weight. "You're a friend of Carl's?" she asked with coy amusement, as if it was both unlikely and unfortunate that such a person should exist. She shook her head and laughed again to indicate that, likely or not, this was fine with her. "Hang on a minute," she added, maneuvering past him onto the porch. "I'll have to get a six-pack."

Ruby disappeared inside and came back with six long necks in their cardboard case. She lifted out two and cracked them open on the porch step. Handing one to Sean, she sat down beside him, so that for the first time they were at the same level. For the first time, she caught the scent that heat and dust turned to on his skin. She took a deep breath of it, rolled it over on her tongue, then took a sip of beer.

"So you know my husband," she said. She looked straight ahead, smiling as if it were just her luck.

"I do," he confirmed. He glanced at her profile and again was granted only half a view of her. "I knew him growing up, but that was back when—"

"How long's it been since you last saw him?" Ruby cut in. Already, she was almost done with her beer.

Sean fanned his fingers out as if they held the time. "God, I don't even know," he said slowly. "Four, five years, I guess." He paused and wondered if he should have answered farther from the truth. "But before that was back in elementary school."

Ruby nodded, though she wasn't concerned with the details. She was concerned instead with the way Sean wet his lips before he spoke, the way his Adam's apple moved. She was concerned with the way, when he was thinking back, the skin crinkled between his eyes.

"So, does Carl ever mention any of us?" Sean questioned, leading her. "Does he ever tell you about any of his old friends?"

Ruby shook her head. "No, not so much," she said. "Not so much as he talks about whiskey and ball games and horse-shit. No hard feelings, though. I'm sure there's plenty good to say about you, but Carl's not really one for conversation. He's more of an eat, drink, burp, shit, sleep kind of guy. And swear, he swears a lot, too. A charming husband." Sean stared at her with a furrowed brow, taken aback, confused.

"But anyway," she said, cupping her hands with the bottle between them. "What brings you here to see my husband?" She surveyed his body for imperfections, any signs of filth or laziness that could help her associate him with Carl.

Sean felt her breath brush the side of his face and expected she might touch him if he moved even one more inch toward her.

"I'm actually looking for work," he said. He chose his words carefully. "I heard there might be something in this area, and then I remembered Carl lived here a long ways back. I didn't know for sure if he'd still be around. In part, this is a surprise."

Ruby laughed at his formality. "Well, in part this is a surprise for me, too," she mocked. "It isn't every day I meet someone who admits to being a friend of Carl's." She put her hand over his thigh as she said it. "I can think of a lot of better ways to make an introduction."

Sean tensed his leg so that under her grip she might feel his response. "Well, you know," he said casually, as if he could ignore what was happening, "I thought it'd be good to come and see how Carl's done for himself. After all these years, I mean. I thought it'd be—"

"How's he done?" She squeezed his leg before he could finish.

"Just fine," he said right away.

"Just fine?" she repeated, and caught onto his gaze with her own before he could look away.

"I'd say he can't complain," he said, and let his whole self tumble into her eyes.

They finished their beers in silence, facing the ridge a far distance in front of them. The orange flicker had grown into a steady line, meandering along the mountain's edge. Eyeing it, Ruby wasn't sure what she had started, only that there seemed much more sense in having him stay than in having him leave. She stood up, pretending that way she could see the fire better. She held her nose in the air, as if from so far away she could breathe in the smoke. When she sat back down, she closed the space between herself and Sean.

"Sorry," she said when her hip bumped his, as if it had been accidental. She made a motion to shift her position.

"No," he said, and she didn't.

"Can't smell it yet." She tilted her chin toward the mountain, her head facing his.

Sean opened his mouth, but stopped short of speaking.

"What?" She tapped her boot on his.

"Nothing," he said. Her eyes were inches from his; he saw her red hair falling down either side of her face. This time there was no dim light, no distance, no need for him to imagine what the other half of her might look like. By now it was hard to remember a time when it had been any different.

"What?" she asked again, bending in closer. "Do you think I don't look at any boys but Carl?"

Sean couldn't answer any more than he could look away.

"Do you think one little afternoon could really come between friends?" she asked. She was watching his lips.

Sean shrugged tentatively, preoccupied with what might happen if either of them leaned any closer. "I don't really know what to—"

"Then don't." Ruby stopped him. "Carl won't be home for a while."

It wasn't deliberate, but their knees were touching, and the tips of Sean's fingers lay more over her knee than his. There was no sense of a logical progression bringing them together, only the fact that from nowhere, they were suddenly no longer apart. Sean moved his tongue between his lips, knowing he should probably open his mouth. He should already have told her why he had come, why they shouldn't be having a beer. Somewhere in his head, he had every good intention. But it seemed there was not enough room between them for a word. And then she leaned into him. He leaned into her. He felt her lips brush his cheek, and in that isolated moment, it seemed only right. It was all he could do to keep his own mouth moving past her cheek to her ear. He raised his head and grazed the tip of her earlobe with his lips.

"I'm Carl's brother. Not a friend," he said, blowing the news into her ear like an eyelash off his fingertip, the whole time wishing it away. "I'm Sean."

Like a twist of smoke, the words fell away in the air. An eerie calm descended. Though only for a matter of seconds, there was no breeze blowing, no fire burning, no breath passing—however faintly—from their lips. Before they pulled apart, both Sean and Ruby could believe that even time itself was stumped as to what to do next. She drew back from him slowly, eyeing him as if she were holding up a brand-new shirt that had just been stained. She was looking to see if the spot, that one ugly detail, could really ruin the rest. It was such a waste, she thought, to see that it could.

"Carl's brother?" She gaped as if he must be mistaken. Carl was in jail. He was out of her life. Those facts alone seemed to make it impossible for Carl's brother to be sitting beside her. Except for Brian, there were no reminders of Carl here. Ruby had made sure of that. She ran the facts through her head again like a checklist. Carl had been in jail for two weeks. Sean hadn't seen him in five years. Carl was five hundred miles away. Sean was so close she had kissed him. *Had tried to kiss him,* she corrected herself. The fact was, she hadn't. On the afternoon he'd come looking for his brother five years later, the fact was that he'd missed him by just two weeks, and by just one second, he had told Ruby who he was too soon.

"You should really work on your timing," she said roughly, breaking the silence.

Sean wet his lips, but Ruby wasn't ready to let him speak.

"No, no, no, no, no." She waved her hands to stop him from trying. She held them up blocking his face so that right that minute nothing new could begin.

It hit her then that this was a man she had already seen with his pants down. It almost struck her as funny. This was a man whose part-naked body she had already seen in her own home. The memory came back to her gradually, until she recalled more precisely how he'd shocked her that afternoon five years ago, how disconcerted she'd felt in the line of his steady stare and its unnerving lack of shame. She remembered how Carl had yelled at her after Sean left, listing all the reasons why Sean deserved to be erased from their lives. He'd yelled as if he could see that Ruby doubted him.

It fascinated Ruby now that timing and circumstance had brought this man back to her front step and that she was not angry with him for concealing, at first, who he was. She was amused by the fact that two weeks after her husband left, this sharper, stronger version of him had been delivered to her door. She smiled at the complicated potential Carl's misfortune had brought her.

"Your timing really couldn't be worse." She smirked, patting his knee. "See, when I said Carl wasn't going to be home for a while, I wasn't kidding."

Sean laughed before he could help himself, then covered his mouth. "I'm sorry," he said, "but I know." He wiped the back of his hand across his lips. "I've talked to Carl."

Ruby straightened up, surprised. "From jail?" she asked, aware that for several weeks she hadn't.

"Yeah, he called me when all this happened. And I admit it, I was pretty surprised to hear from him."

"You're surprised," Ruby said, eyebrows raised.

"Because, you know, Carl and I have never exactly been so brotherly, and I haven't seen him since the last time I . . . since I . . ." He fumbled, unsure how to finish. "Well, since I—"

"I remember," Ruby said, and gave him a good smack on the back as if he might be choking. She smiled to see him squirm again. "I remember well," she emphasized, all big teeth.

Sean tried to swallow his own smile. It didn't strike him as the most appropriate time to joke. And yet it did seem inevitable that they should end up laughing at the bizarre memory they shared, even if there was something less than upright about sitting so close and keeping company this easily now that they each knew who the other was.

"Anyway," Sean said, "I haven't seen him since . . . then, but he called because I guess there's something he wants me to have now that he's away. He said that he wanted me to come get it. So I came, that's why I'm here."

Ruby pursed her lips, trying to guess what it could be. "Well, I hope he said what it is," she said flippantly, " 'cause I sure as hell can't think of a thing in there worth your trouble." She thrust her thumb over her shoulder toward the house. "I hope you haven't been sent on a goose chase."

"No, no, he told me," Sean said. "I'm here to get Evelyn."

"Evelyn?" Ruby straightened up, incredulous.

"He keeps her down at the corral?" Sean went on. "That's what he told me. She belonged to both of us as kids, you know, until we got split up, and now he wants me to have her again, because really she *was,* or I guess *is,* both of ours. And he said she's pregnant. Anyway, he wants me to have her, so that's why I'm here, is to get her."

Ruby appeared confused. "You're really here for Evelyn?"

"Carl said you might not be too happy about it," he answered. "He said you'd always wanted to have her for yourself."

Ruby spat out a laugh to show him nothing could be more ludicrous. "He really thinks that," she said, shaking her head as if until right then she'd forgotten how funny it was. "I don't want Evelyn any more than I want a splinter in my ass, Sean. That horse is old and swayed and has more flies on her back than a year's worth of sticky tape hanging over a greasy gas grill in a diner. All she was good for was giving Carl a hard time. Just another way to get to him. Hell, if you really want her, she's all yours."

Sean nodded vaguely, but he was still contemplating the

sound of his name on her lips. He liked the familiarity it implied. "Well, okay, then." He hesitated. "I guess Carl's idea was for me to stay around here until that foal's born—"

"That'll be weeks," Ruby broke in.

"Yeah," he said, acknowledging that this might be awkward. "I suppose so."

"So are you moving in?" She asked, referring to his truck, to the duffel sitting upright in the passenger seat. She didn't attempt to cushion the question.

Sean turned to her immediately. "Oh, no, no," he said fast, as if nothing could be more obvious. "I mean, I have my truck, and my trailer, and I'll be hanging around town until the foal comes, so I just thought I should let you know that I'm here. That I'll be here." He paused, but she said nothing. "And then I guess I'll have to see how Evelyn's doing after the foal's born," he added, filling the silence. "If she's even worth the trip back, I mean. But I'll take the foal with me, either way. I think that's how Carl wanted it."

Ruby smoothed her hands over her thighs as if she were finished listening. "Fine," she said. She stood up and waited for Sean to do the same.

"Okay," he said, rising. They were almost eye to eye, Sean only slightly taller than she. He thought she seemed distracted. "Hey, I apologize if this isn't the best timing, or situation, or whatever," he said.

"No," she said, shrugging her shoulders, half smiling. "I was just thinking that it's funny."

"What?" he asked, shifting his weight, pushing one hand in his pants pocket.

"That out of the blue I come home to the best tall, dark, and handsome I've seen in too long to remember," she said, "and he just wants my horse." She stared at him long enough to let him know that, whether or not it should be, this was something more than funny.

He returned her stare to let her know that even if he shouldn't, he agreed. "I don't know, though," he said, matching her half smile. "Evelyn was a pretty attractive young lady from what I remember." He took a step away, getting ready to leave.

Ruby wasn't sure, but she thought he winked at her.

"Yeah, and from what I remember—" she started, dropping her eyes to Sean's zipper.

"Hey," he objected, wheeling around so she could only fix on his behind. "That's enough." He laughed over his shoulder, walking toward his truck.

"You bet it is," she called to him before she turned to go inside. She was still grinning when she opened the screen door. She jumped backwards when she found Brian standing just inside it.

"And what do you think you're doing, little man?" she asked, bending down. At any other time she would have snapped at him for spying, but he'd caught her all wound up in a different set of thoughts.

"Watching the fire like you told me," he said meekly, arms stiff at his sides.

"Oh, yeah?" she said, pretending to believe him. She scooped him up in her arms and held him in front of her, a sign of affection she didn't show every day. "And what do you think?" she asked. "What's it gonna be this year?"

"That man was Daddy's brother?" he asked as if he hadn't heard her. She stood him back down on the floor and thought twice about what to say.

"Yeah, Bri," she replied more gently, keeping her hands on his shoulders. "That was Daddy's brother. He's going to be here for a while." She squatted down to his level and pushed his hair off his forehead. "What do you think of that?"

Brian gawked at her as if there were only one right answer and, however hard he might try, he wouldn't find it. His brow wrinkled as if he might cry. But he didn't know if it was right or wrong to feel happy at the prospect of meeting his father's brother—a man who was only kind of like his father, a man his father didn't care for. He couldn't hold it all in his head long enough to find the answer. He was eight years old. He missed his father. His father was in jail. He gazed past Ruby blankly, letting these thoughts wash over him. Even through the screen, he could still make out the fire.

"I think it'll be the biggest one yet," he said solemnly, his eyes relaxed and lazy as if the flames were right there in front of him. Whether or not a fire ever came, it was the same thing he said every year.

Ruby tousled his hair. "You," she groaned as if he had been teasing her.

She climbed the stairs to her bedroom and peered out the window to the driveway. Sean's truck was pulling onto the road toward town. The empty horse trailer swung along behind it, kicking up dirt like smoke. Ruby kept her eye on it until the trailer disappeared behind clouds of dust, and then she turned and leaned her shoulder blades against the window.

"Evelyn." She laughed aloud, resting her head back on the pane. She put one hand over her face and closed her eyes against the notion that the creature should have been good for something after all. "Evelyn," she repeated under her breath, this time as if answering a question. "Who'd of thought."

Evelyn was standing in the corral, in the corner farthest
from the feed and the water trough, as she always did.
She had her backside to the other horses and the wranglers
in the office, as if she understood the statement she was
making. She was bored with them, she didn't need their company. The early sun beat down on her through the thin film
of smoke in the air, so that her long, bowed neck and swayed
back seemed to droop to the ground under its weight—
though the fact was, sun or no sun, Evelyn never stood in
the corral any differently. She always looked as though she
were slouching. Even as a young horse, Evelyn's slumped

body and sleepy eyes had seemed to be explaining how she'd known, ever since the day she was born, just how tough a world she'd come into. She stood with her hooves unnaturally far apart like a tired old woman doing all she could to keep her balance. In the corner of the corral, moving only her tail to swipe at flies, she appeared to be always taking herself too seriously.

But really Carl was the only one who took her too seriously. The other wranglers liked having Evelyn around as a general source of comedy, but Carl watched over her as he would his own child. He had the ability to overlook Evelyn's sweeping flaws as only a parent would, and in return, Evelyn kept alive for Carl the few memories he retained of having two parents, a brother, one roof. Always he defended her to the other wranglers, reasoning that she stood so far from the rest of the horses simply because that was the spot where he regularly treated her to the special mix of feed and carrots that his little girl deserved.

The morning after Sean arrived in Whitticker, Brian stood by Evelyn's usual spot with a pail full of feed he'd scooped from Carl's sack of special mix. The pail was heavy in his arms, and he placed it on the dirt, squatting beside it. He poked his fingers through the grains to identify the different ingredients, wondering what to do when the last of it was gone. He ached all over from waking so early again—riding his bike to the corral for the fifteenth morning in a row— and the air tasted dirty to him, laced with smoke. But he knew his dad would have been up this early if he'd been home, and someone needed to feed Evelyn now that he was gone. And not just regular feed like the other wranglers would give her if Brian didn't come. Brian felt no warmer toward Evelyn than he did toward any other horse, but she was the only part of his father he could still put his hands on. These mornings, he liked to envision the day he might be able to tell his dad how Evelyn was doing fine, how he'd taken care of her just right. He liked to think his father might someday look at him and see that he was becoming responsible—that in his father's absence, he was growing up. Brian scooped the seed with his cupped palms and, holding it out through the fence toward Evelyn, felt himself of some importance.

Evelyn didn't come to him right away, but once there she pushed her mouth hard into his palms, spraying the feed as she smacked at it with her awkward, floppy lips. Brian knew he could have hung the pail from the fence post just as easily, but he liked feeling Evelyn's soft, thick lips nuzzling his palms for more. In his hands, they tickled. Only when he saw the wranglers' office door open at the other end of the corral did Brian pull his hands away and hang the pail on the post. He climbed up onto the the fence, pulling himself against the railings so he could better view the office.

There were three men coming out of the door, shaking hands and slapping backs. They adjusted their hats and laughed loudly, showing what a good visit they'd had. Brian had never spent enough time at the corral to know more than a few of the men his father worked with, and he wasn't

sure he recognized any of these three. He could make out
that two of them were addressing the third, both shaking his
hand but not each other's. The third man Brian felt fairly
sure he knew. He had seen him just once, the day before,
but simply the breadth of this man's shoulders and the way
he backpedaled as he said good-bye was enough for Brian
to know that it was Sean. He was giving a wave to the two
men as he headed toward Brian's end of the corral. Brian
checked over his shoulder in the other direction and saw
Sean's truck and horse trailer in the parking lot, same as
they'd been in his driveway the day before. He couldn't believe he hadn't noticed them earlier.

Sean was striding quickly toward him, eyes on the ground,
hat down low on his head. Brian jumped down off the fence
and planted himself in Sean's path. He crossed his arms over
his chest, then dropped them to his sides. He had lain awake
the night before thinking of different ways he might introduce himself to Sean. He imagined how his mother might
push him forward by his shoulders as if he were a little boy.
And he pictured how he would shrug her hands off and stand
up straight, nod his head hello like a man. But in all the ways
he'd visualized it, he'd never imagined that Ruby wouldn't be
right there beside him.

Brian took one step forward, into Sean's view. Sean halted
and reversed a step, surprised that he was suddenly so close
to crashing into something. He laughed to see that it was
just a boy.

"Well, good morning to you," he said, grasping Brian's

shoulder to keep the two of them from colliding. He pushed off Brian's body as he circled around him to keep on going.

A sharp pang hollowed Brian's stomach, but he did his best not to take it as rejection. He simply hadn't considered that Sean might not remember him, and he barely hesitated a second before spinning around to face Sean's back.

"Sean," he called nervously. "Hi." He feared he sounded even younger than he was, nothing like a man. He raised his hand above his belt in a premature wave at Sean's backside.

Sean whirled around and took off his hat. He hunched over toward Brian, his hands on his knees. "Did you say something to me?" he asked.

Brian could not find the voice to answer. Instead, he stood wide-eyed, awed by the size of Sean's face so close to his own. From behind the screen door yesterday, he'd seen no more than that Sean was tall and strong and with his mother, three indications to Brian that Sean might be like his father. But up close, Sean's smile was easier, and his eyes more alive, than Carl's had ever been. His skin was rough, not worn. Brian was surprised that this was the same person he'd seen talking to his mother, the same person he hoped would stick around to remind him of his father. Sean seemed like no other man he'd known. Unlike the wranglers Brian had met with Carl, Sean did not move with that haggard drag Brian had come to assume was part of growing into an adult. Even Sean's footprints in the sand, Brian noticed, were larger and deeper than most. Brian's eyes followed each footstep right back to where Sean crouched in front of him, right up his body from his boots to his face. He examined Sean's features again, marveling that this new man in town was a part of his own family.

Sean rose up as if he wasn't going to wait for an answer, but before he could leave, Brian thrust his hand forward, unsure where to hold it because he had never been the first to offer a hand before. And though the gesture felt unnatural to him, it made him feel considerably more grown-up. He pulled his shoulders back the way he'd wanted to from the start, and raised his hand higher as he advanced toward Sean.

"I'm Brian," he said louder than before. "My dad's your brother."

"Brian," Sean exhaled immediately. He opened his arms to hug him, but stopped when he saw that Brian still held his hand out for a shake. He leaned back so that they could meet, as he could see Brian wanted, man to man. "Hi, Brian," he said, taking his hand. "I've heard all about you from your dad. It's good to finally meet you."

Brian looked down and blushed at Sean's boots, unable to be as formal as he'd intended. He'd planned to ask Sean how his drive from New Mexico had been, if there was anything he could do for him, how he liked Whitticker so far. "Are you going to stay with us?" he eagerly asked instead, raising his eyes to the tarnish on Sean's belt buckle, the lines on his hands. In front of him like that, Brian found each detail so impressive.

"I'm going to be in town for a while," Sean said as he

put a boot up on the fence railing. "Did your mom tell you that?"

"Yeah," Brian said, and followed Sean to the fence. He climbed up where he had been before. They both looked to Evelyn.

"Did she tell you that I'm here to take this one home with me?" He stretched his hand out to pat Evelyn's muzzle.

"No, but I heard," Brian said. He loved how easily Sean's hand cupped Evelyn's nose. "I heard you tell my mom that you talked to my dad."

Sean cocked his head, pretending to be impressed. He reached his other hand out to stroke Evelyn's neck, but she jerked away from him. "You have some good ears, don't you?" he joked, cupping his hand over Brian's shoulder instead.

"Yes," Brian said curtly, still waiting for an answer.

Sean inched closer to Brian. "Yeah, I talked to your dad," he said, lowering his voice. "And you know what?" He bent down, not quite sure how to speak to a child.

"No, because I haven't talked to him," Brian said, a conspicuous edge in his voice.

Sean tried to remember being Brian's age. He wondered if he himself had been anywhere near as composed at eight years old. He wanted to know how a boy a fraction of his own age could make him question himself as he hadn't before; he couldn't think what to say.

He cleared his throat. "He sounds okay, Brian. I mean, of course he wants to be back here with you and your mom—"

"Did he say that?" Brian cut him off.

Sean tried his best not to hesitate. "Of course that's what he wants, Brian, but for now he's got to get through what he's got to get through, you know? And so he called to talk to me about making sure that somebody would take care of Evelyn and her little foal, but it looks like he didn't have anything to worry about, did he?"

Again, Brian couldn't keep from smiling. He shook his head. "And I don't even really like horses," he said, as if to impress Sean with how perfectly Evelyn would have been cared for if, in fact, he did.

Sean was encouraged that he had picked the right thing to say. He leapt back away from the fence dramatically to bolster Brian's enthusiasm. "Carl's your daddy, and you don't really like horses?" He exaggerated his surprise, mussing Brian's hair.

"No. I like swimming," Brian offered, matter of fact, his smile fading because swimming was serious. "And my mom doesn't like it really, but she drives me anyway."

Sean looked at Brian as if he didn't follow.

"It's the same thing," he explained. "Even though I don't like horses, I'm going to take care of Evelyn right while my dad's in—" he stumbled, not wanting to finish his sentence. "While my dad's gone," he said quietly.

"Well, all right." Sean nodded. He reached out for Evelyn, embarrassed that in front of a boy so young he should feel a nervous need to occupy his hands. "That's very mature of you, Brian. I think you're the oldest eight-year-old I've ever met."

"Yeah, I know," Brian said. "My Middies teacher, Sherley Wadlow, she says so, too. And I'm the youngest in the group." He studied Sean for his reaction. He was starting to think that he liked this man. "So are you staying with us?" he asked again.

Sean checked the corral to see if anyone was near enough to hear them. "That's not my decision to make, Brian," he said. "You tell your mother that decision's up to her. And it's up to you, too, of course. It's up to both of you." He was glad to get a chance to slip it in. He wanted to make sure Ruby would hear about this meeting. "I'll bc here until that foal's born, anyway," he added. "Are you and your mom going to be mad at me when I take it away?"

Brian shrugged his shoulders. "I don't care," he said.

Sean wanted to know if Ruby would. He noticed Brian move to take the feed pail off the post.

"Did you know that your dad and I watched when Evelyn was born?" Sean asked, to keep Brian there a little longer.

Brian shook his head.

"Yeah, when your dad wasn't so much older than you," he said. He saw that Brian was listening. "And he and I watched from behind the stall fence while our dad was in there getting Evelyn out. Dad had to stick his arm right inside our mare to help her, all the way in, so it looked like he only had one arm." Sean held one arm out in front of him to demonstrate.

"Gross." Brian shuddered and wrinkled up his face.

"Yeah, that's what I thought, too," Sean said. "I didn't want to go near that stall, and my mom had to hold on to me so I wouldn't cry, because I was afraid that our mare might be dying. But your dad knew what was going on the whole time, and he climbed right through the fence and went in there. Nobody could've stopped him. And when Evelyn came out, your dad was right there with both arms around her. He picked her up and put her on her own feet for the first time and held her little legs so she could keep her balance. They were like toothpicks. And everybody at the corral cheered for her being born, and for your dad there holding her up and being all covered in goop and grinning so big his cheeks practically swallowed his eyes." Sean paused, looking at Evelyn as if he could see her birth right there in front of him. "From that day on," he said, "I think Evelyn always liked Carl best, even if she was supposed to be both of ours."

Brian followed Sean's gaze, trying to see the story as best he could. "And people were cheering for my dad?" he asked, to hear Sean say it again. He was beaming.

"Hell, yes," Sean said. "Every one of them."

Brian continued to gaze ahead, miles and years away. He was picturing Carl at the corral doing all things that were good and important and praiseworthy. He saw him fixing a saddle, feeding a foal, winning a barrel race with a bright-colored bandanna at his neck. He saw him leaning over the fence to kiss Ruby. "Tell me something else about my dad," he said. He wanted more reasons to feel proud.

"All right. How about we go downtown and get some breakfast," Sean suggested, hopeful about the idea, "and then I will." Ruby would surely hear about their meeting if they went downtown.

Brian's face suddenly snapped back into the present and turned unsure. Sean wondered if he had said too much.

Brian tugged on his fingers. "I ate a doughnut already," he said as if that ruined the plans. He spoke as he would to a stranger.

"That's okay," Sean said, backing off.

"I should finish feeding Evelyn," Brian said, stepping toward the fence.

Sean moved out of his way. "All right," he said, digging into his pocket for his keys, wishing he'd been more patient. "I'm going to go get myself some eggs, then. You think there's a place around here that can feed me as well as you feed Evelyn?"

It was enough to make Brian smile again. "The Early Bird," he answered. "By the post office. But you have to ask for ketchup in the mornings because it's not on the tables until lunch. If you like it on eggs," he said, bashful for having said more than he needed.

"Thanks," Sean said. "I can't have them any other way." He gave Brian a quick pat on the shoulder. "I'll see you later, then, Brian, okay?"

It flattered Brian that Sean had phrased it as a question. "Yeah," he replied, without meeting Sean's eyes. "I'll see you." And before Sean could turn to leave, Brian was up on the top fence rail, watching Evelyn feed. If he heard the crunch of Sean's footsteps moving away, he didn't let on. All he was thinking as he watched Evelyn was that he'd talked to Sean, his father's brother, and that he'd done it pretty well. He was thinking he most certainly was the oldest eight-year-old he knew, and that it was going to be a better day than he had ever guessed.

Maybe the one thing that could have been better, Brian thought, was the weather. The smoke from Firehouse Hill had settled into town during the night and changed the look of the land, so that the whole area, through a hazy film, seemed out of focus to him. Every breath he took reminded him that the hill was burning, as the smoke caught and stung in his throat. Biking home, he passed only a few other people in the center of town. They were either coming or going, with hands over their mouths; nobody was just standing around in the murky air. Brian knew he should have ridden directly home, but to him the fire signified more than the dryness it left in his throat. Something impressive was happening in his town where noteworthy events rarely did, and he wanted to watch up close. So where he should have turned off the main road to head home, Brian instead pedaled straight until he picked up the dirt path leading to the base of Firehouse Hill.

A cluster of firefighters in yellow was gathered at the site, and Brian stopped short so he wouldn't be told to leave. In the past, the fighters hadn't been called to work until at least two days into the fire, so Brian thought perhaps he'd been right, that this fire would be the biggest one yet. He looked to the sky where a helicopter approached the burning terrain to dump water. He watched its propeller slip in and out of sight as it dipped and swayed through the smoke.

The fire had moved a good distance overnight, extending a second line of flames down off the ridge and across the front of Firehouse Hill to form a fat, glowing ring around the hill's belly. The actual flames were barely distinguishable through the smoke, but as Brian strained to see, he could make out the progress of the blaze. He watched as a flame leapt up and over a small rise, racing down the slope like a cowboy on horseback. The motion made him think of Sean. He imagined Sean riding with the same swift and reckless certainty through the scrub and cacti in his path. Brian followed the branch of flames as it tumbled down the hill, and even in the heat, he felt goose bumps rising on his arms. He couldn't hold still with his excitement over Sean's arrival, the fire's return, the sense that things were just beginning. It was all he could do to keep from bursting as he rode home. He could hardly wait to tell Ruby about his morning at the corral.

She was still fast asleep when he peeled into their driveway. Even though it was nearly noon and he was beside himself, he didn't dare wake her. Brian had gone to bed at nine o'clock the night before, listening to the watery jangle of Ruby washing dinner dishes in the kitchen below. He had always liked falling asleep to the sound of his parents moving around their house, creaking up and down the stairs, talking in full voices to each other, with all the lights on except for Brian's bedroom lamp. But long after drifting to sleep, Brian had been awakened several times by Ruby's heavy footsteps pounding between her bedroom and the kitchen. He'd heard her slam the refrigerator door more than once and knew she wouldn't have made enough noise to wake him had she not been drinking. The last time Brian checked the clock, it read one-nineteen A.M. He'd slept through the rest of the night, but when he rose in the morning to feed Evelyn, he was careful not to wake his mother because he knew that she'd been up late.

The truth was, Ruby had stayed up most of the night. She had finished the beers she and Sean had left untouched, and as each sip went to her head, thoughts of Sean spun around inside her, so that she couldn't lie down, much less fall asleep. Instead, she sat up with the moon, hoping enough sips would bring her one good reason why it was all right to be thinking about her husband's brother this way. When he'd been sitting with her on the porch, she hadn't needed even one reason why. It had all seemed so clear then, before the sun set and she had started thinking; she was alone, he was here, Carl would never have to know.

But it wasn't until after noon that Ruby saw daylight again and lifted herself out of bed. In jeans she'd never taken off the night before, she stumbled over an almost empty bottle and held her head as the smell of stale beer rose up from the floor. She swallowed two aspirin, then pulled her hair back in a ponytail, making a point not to look in the mirror. "No thank you," she said in its direction.

Ruby went downstairs into the kitchen and opened the back door. She looked across the yard to Brian. He was squatting in the corner with his back to her, hands on his face, inspecting a hill of ants. When the door clapped shut behind Ruby, he hopped up and kicked his sneaker through the mound of sand.

"Morning," he said, facing her, looking at his watch.

"I know it's not morning," she said back, hands on her hips. She squinted her eyes and winced toward the sun. She guessed it was close to one o'clock. "I'm going into town," she said, rubbing one eye. "Is there somewhere you want to go?"

"I have a bike," Brian said. He sprinted over to the bottom of the steps. "I already went downtown." He rocked from heel to toe.

She grimaced down at him as if to question whose son he really was. "What?" she asked him, swinging open the back door. "Do you want an award or something? You went downtown."

Ruby often regretted the moments when she was short with Brian, but she couldn't always summon the patience to deal with his cryptic expressions and oddball behavior. She would chide herself, each time she directed another caustic string of words at him, that a better mother would learn to hold her tongue. But she was also secretly impressed at the way Brian seemed to brush off her curt snaps as if he'd hardly heard them, as if he almost understood that his mother had this weakness she couldn't be bothered to control.

"I went to the corral to feed Evelyn," he reminded her, unfazed, his eyebrows peaked. He was trying to lead her.

Ruby raised her eyebrows, too, to show him how ridiculous he looked to her. "Well, thank you very much," she said. "Aren't you responsible. Now I'm going downtown to get some food in me. If you go anywhere else, leave a note." She headed toward the kitchen. "And don't stay out all day in this smoke," she added. "You'll turn your insides black."

Brian was accustomed to her brusqueness, though it sometimes still made him flinch. He hesitated before running up the steps after her, catching the screen door just before it shut. "I talked to Sean," he announced, sliding through the small opening.

The name was hardly off Brian's lips before Ruby twirled around and marched back to where he poked his head into the kitchen. Swinging the door open again, she ran them both out into the sunlight. "Daddy's brother, Sean?" she asked aggressively.

113

"Yeah." Brian nodded, grinning from ear to ear. "At the corral when I was—"

"And you talked to him?" she said demandingly, but it was nothing Brian wasn't used to. He took it to be her own excitement, and he felt goose bumps tingling on his arms again.

"Yeah," he started up. "He was coming around the side where I was feeding Evelyn, and I jumped out in front of him and said hi, and he stopped, and I put my hand out, and he shook it." Brian could hardly keep up with his words.

"And what did he say?" she asked. She spoke calmly because she could see that Brian was all wound up. She was afraid if he grew too excited, he'd forget something, and she needed to hear everything just right.

"He told me about Dad and how he was the hero and all the people cheered for him when Evelyn was born. How ever since that day, Evelyn's always liked Dad best," Brian said. He was glowing.

"Yeah, that's right." Ruby tried again to slow him down. "That's a good story, isn't it?" She put her hand over his head and smoothed his hair. "Your dad was really great with Evelyn," she said, and knelt in front of him. "But is that all he said, Bri, just about Evelyn?" She needed an answer. "Did he say anything about you—or me?" she asked.

Brian pouted, trying to remember. He thought there had been something. "I'm not sure," he replied. "But he said I'm the oldest eight-year-old he's ever met." Brian's face was lit with pride, but Ruby's expression had cooled down considerably. It seemed Sean hadn't told Brian anything of interest to her, and so she straightened up and made for the door.

"Oh, but I know." Brian remembered just as she was about to disappear. He held a finger up in the air. "He said one thing to tell you. He said it's up to you if he can stay here." He could see Ruby staring at him over her shoulder. "And he said it's part up to me, too, Mom, and I think he should." He was nodding his head. "I do."

Ruby's smile showed not so much that she was happy, as that she was relieved. "You do, do you?" She laughed.

"I really do, Mom," he said, also relieved to see his mother happy.

"Well, okay, then," she said, turning to leave for sure this time. "We'll see if we can track him down." She let the screen door slam shut and moved briskly through the house, out the front door, and onto the porch. She took a deep breath and thought she might finally have found the good reason she'd spent all night looking for: she was alone, Sean was here, *and Brian wanted to be close to him, too.*

Ruby hadn't considered earlier that Brian might have been a reason for her reservations about Sean. She had never hesitated for Brian's sake in the past when her attention had drifted from Carl to other men. But noticing now how Brian lit up over shaking Sean's hand, Ruby concluded that of course it was fine to bring Sean home. Had that clarity lasted, she wouldn't have thought twice about inviting him. But perhaps it was the smoke in the air, or too many beers the night before, that made things seem foggy again to Ruby all too quickly. From the porch, Buzzard Peak was no longer visible. Even right in front of her, the truck in the driveway, the saguaro on the hill beyond their yard, were blurred. It was as if everything around her had lost its edge. And as much as she would rather have seen clearly right then, Ruby marveled nevertheless that a phenomenon so threatening as fire could have such a dulling effect. She felt hazy herself as she got into her truck and headed for town.

Ruby drove to Bar 4 because it was as good a place as any to spend the day indoors. She figured it was the most likely spot where everyone would gather to escape the smoky air. Whenever a fire came to town, people liked to pull up a stool to a pitcher of beer and a line of frosty glasses and discuss with anyone else around their predictions about the fire's impact. Those who had lived in Whitticker for many years cited past fires by date and duration and consequence, and they tended to take it personally when other people's opinions differed from their own. Ruby had seen debates grow heated in the course of a night, especially if there was a volunteer firefighter in the bar who'd actually had experience controlling a blaze. Plenty of Whitticker residents had been certified as volunteer fighters at one time or another, but only a handful had ever been called to assist the full-time firemen who kept their bags packed during fire season, ready to pounce on any flame that sparked within their designated territory. Given enough time on a stool at Bar 4, however, it seemed everyone—experienced or not—became an authority on the fire.

Bar 4 was cavernous and dark inside, with no particular decor. The floor and stools and tables were all made of the same dark, thick oak, and the few lights on the ceiling were unshaded, bare bulbs. At the far end of the room was a pool table and a dartboard; in the front ran a long, battered bar with beer logos on the mirrors above it. Posters of beer girls in bathing suits hung by the bathrooms. Most of the time, only men claimed the stools at the bar.

In the years Ruby had been going there, she'd almost never paid for a drink. She knew the bartenders and the regulars and the two line-cooks in the kitchen. Anybody she didn't know still knew something about her. There were few places she liked better to walk into than Bar 4.

That afternoon, the bar was already as crowded as it usually was after dinner. A group of wranglers who used to work with Carl at the Flying C stood at the bar, and Ruby guessed they might have run the horses to pasture and quit early because of the smoke. One of them waved her over as soon as she opened the door.

"Rub!" he shouted, and gave her a sloppy whack on her shoulder. He had clearly been there awhile.

"Hey, Mitch," she said, steadying him with her arms. She ran her eyes across the rest of them and added, "Hi, boys."

After a chorus of greetings, Lyle Fredericks broke forward from the group and put his arm around Ruby. Lyle, too, had worked with Carl, but he and Ruby had been friends long before Carl came to town. They'd grown up sharing the same homerooms at Eagle Watch Elementary and lived down the road from each other until they were nine, when Lyle's grandmother died and left her big house in town to his family. Lyle had spent two weeks living at Ruby's house after his family moved because he said he would never live in a place where a dead person had been. He and Ruby had been friends for as long as she could remember.

"Afternoon, Rub," he said, giving her whole body a squeeze. He was burly but soft, and Ruby liked how his embrace always warmed her. "Looks like you just rolled out of bed."

She tugged at her ponytail and wished she'd looked in the mirror after all. "It was one of those nights," she said feebly.

"Yeah," he said, raising his beer. "It was one of those days." He removed his arm and took a sip. "Actually, Rub, I wanted to ask you—"

"Ruby needs a beer!" Mitch shouted, reeling toward the bar. Seconds later, he shoved a glass at her. Ruby didn't have time to thank him before he'd stumbled toward the bar and stood with both feet unsteadily on the rungs of a stool, so that he rose up heads above the crowd. "A toast to Ruby!" he bellowed, teetering. "Raise 'em up," he yelled until he got more attention.

"Mitch, hang on," Lyle interrupted, trying to stop him.

"To Ruby!" Mitch called again. "There's no one can have a pair of shoes filled—"

"Come on, Mitch," Lyle insisted.

"There's no one can have a pair of shoes filled faster!" Mitch finished, tumbling backwards, guzzling his beer.

Ruby grabbed Lyle by his shirt. "What the hell is that supposed to mean?" she asked, knowing full well, of course, but not exactly why.

"Nothing," he said, watching Mitch. "Someone should take him home."

"No, don't be like that," she said sharply, slapping his hip. "Tell me what's going on."

Lyle shrugged his shoulders. "I guess it's nothing you don't know about," he answered. He beckoned her away from the other wranglers to the side wall, and Ruby followed. "We just never knew that Carl had a brother. That's all."

"What do you know about Sean?" she demanded, lowering her voice.

"Hey, nothing until a few hours ago," Lyle said. "But he showed up at the corral at the crack of dawn today asking about a job, and Mel showed him around. Nobody knew who he was. He said he was moving to town, and then he talked for the better part of an hour like there's no stable he can't run with his eyes closed. I think it would of put some of the guys off more, except it seems like he's right. In all the years I've worked ranches, I've never seen anybody take a bunch of horses he doesn't know like that and—"

"So Mel gave him the job?" Ruby cut him short.

"Just like that." He snapped his fingers. "I admit, he'd of been crazy not to. You should've seen the way Sean marched in there all business, all serious, same as Carl. Like Carl never left. That's all Mitch meant by that. That it feels kind of strange to have his place filled so fast. And then to have Sean tell us as he's leaving that he's Carl's brother. Like it slipped his mind until right then. When I'm not sure all the guys even knew, or at least remembered, that Carl had a brother at all. I don't know. That's a lot for one day." Lyle paused, surveying the bar again. "Enough for Mitch, anyway. But that's some houseguest, Rub."

Ruby had locked her knees, tense, and she felt herself growing light-headed. "What makes you think he's staying with me?" she retorted. It was supposed to be a decision she would make by herself.

"Well, who else would he be staying with?" Lyle asked, as if there were nothing more obvious. "One of them?" He cocked his head over Ruby's shoulder toward the rear of the room. To her disbelief, Ruby saw Sean standing on the far side of the pool table, surrounded by women.

"My God," she whispered.

"Yeah," she hardly heard Lyle agree, "it's really something else."

Sean held a bottle of beer in one hand and a pool cue in

121

the other. Ruby could make out a blue kerchief tied around his neck and a cigarette in the corner of his mouth. She observed in him the same rugged manner she'd been drawn to the day before, when he was a stranger and they were alone on her porch. Beyond that, though, she was surprised by how little else about him seemed the same. He was all big hand gestures, all big laughs, while he shot pool with another wrangler from the Flying C. Ruby counted seven women at the pool table, each taking in Sean's actions as if they had been dipped in gold. She noted how tall he stood, how fluidly he swaggered alongside the table for a shot.

She saw that Sean was comfortable. That was the difference. Sean had a job now; he was moving into town; now this was his bar, too. As a man, as a wrangler, as the new arrival in town—as anyone *other* than Carl's brother on her doorstep—he must always be this way: smooth and steady and comfortable. Only a few hours after they had met him, these wranglers seemed in agreement that Sean was the most skilled horseman they had ever watched work. Ruby saw how these women were going out of their way to stand at his side. In one day, Sean had garnered more respect than Carl had ever earned, and more attention than Ruby generally received. Brian was showing more interest in him than anyone else he'd met as far back as she could remember. Sean was moving in fast, and on top of it all, only one day after he'd rolled into town, after she had tried to kiss him, people already assumed he was living with her.

True or not, Ruby wanted to show them who Sean's closest tie to their town really was. She swallowed half her beer and handed the glass to Lyle. "I'll see you," she said bluntly and headed for the pool table. Sean was leaning over it, concentrating on a shot as if oblivious to the number of eyes on him.

"Watch out," Ruby said to the women hanging around Sean. Raising her hands in the air in front of her, she parted his audience down the middle and took her place to his side. But still Sean didn't seem to notice.

Ruby tossed her head back, swinging her ponytail and sweeping a few loose, messy hairs from her face. Her shoulders were high and squared, as always. "Looks like you're making yourself right at home," she said. The bite in her voice carried more than a subtle suggestion of challenge. She hadn't waited for Sean to take his shot. He was bent over the table with his stomach almost against the felt, running the cue back and forth through his fingers in measured, preparatory strokes. If he heard her, he didn't let on.

"I said, you're really moving right on in, aren't you?" she repeated, her voice strident. She was well aware of the eyes on her.

"Hold on," he said distractedly under his breath, ready to shoot. This time it was he who didn't realize to whom he was speaking. His shot cracked, and the balls raced swiftly, exactly as he wanted them. There was a murmur of approval from his audience.

"Now, who was that who thought they could make me miss?" He laughed, straightening up. He scanned the table and stopped himself short. "Ruby," he blurted, his voice entirely changed. He gave her a smile so natural that he had only himself to blame for compromising his demeanor. He put the cue stick down.

"Hey, Sean," she said, and with her single nod a whole new game had begun. The other wrangler retreated from the table and whispered to the women at his side. Ruby saw she had underestimated the size of the group that was forming to witness her public meeting with Sean. Their awe was as palpable to her as their physical presence. And awe was nothing new to Ruby. She had been scrutinized like this for as long as she could remember. In truth, she liked having all eyes on her. So much attention couldn't help but be empowering, except that this time, even as she was being looked at, she was looking at Sean the same way.

If it were possible, Ruby found Sean dangerously more attractive in this new setting than on her doorstep. Maybe it wasn't yet entirely his town, but that pool cue and that bottle were his tools, this smoky room his most familiar environment. She saw him on a different scale from any other man she'd known. It didn't take much looking to find a larger store of life inside him than she was accustomed to seeing in the men around Whitticker.

With the murmur diminishing, Ruby felt a pressure to perform. "I would have thought you could do two things at once," she said. "I was saying how you've really made yourself at home."

Sean, too, assessed the crowd around him. "Here's as good as I've found," he said back at her eyes. "The front seat of a truck loses its appeal after a while." He was close to outright flirting.

Ruby's eyes circled the room. "You've found everybody's home away from home in this place," she said, grinning, inviting the crowd into their conversation. Those who were willing to admit that they were listening laughed, and Ruby was taken aback by how loud the reaction was. She thought it would be wiser to keep this exchange private, and she stepped closer to ask Sean to follow her outside.

"I met Brian this morning," he said quietly, before she could. Five words and he narrowed the conversation to the two of them, pushing their audience from his sight.

Ruby shuffled her feet and wished that he had waited. She reminded herself that only in her head had the two of them become more than harmless, but she felt she had lost some control of the conversation at Sean's mention of Brian. She couldn't tell him to shut up, to take their talk outside, when he was merely chatting about her son. But she had an uneasy sense of where he was leading, and she would have far preferred to continue out of earshot of anyone else around them. "He told me," was all she said.

"He's a very grown-up kid," Sean continued in a normal tone of voice. "I've never met a kid so old," he said, leaning against the pool table.

She watched his thigh spread on the table's wooden rim, and she shifted her position closer to him to block any lingering bystanders from her view. "I know it," she said.

He bowed his head to make sure he had her eyes. "So what did he tell you?" he whispered.

"That his daddy is a hero," she responded emphatically, loud enough to be overheard. They both hesitated, until she laughed as if something were absurd. But she didn't know for sure if the absurdity was Carl being called a hero, or herself and Sean dancing around each other with awkward bits of conversation in a room full of people who knew that, hero or no hero, Carl was her husband, Sean her husband's brother.

"Yeah, I told him that story about Evelyn." He paused. "Is that all Brian told you?"

She knew what he was getting at, and she shot him a look to say, *I'm with you, but hang on.* She couldn't bear that someone might be listening. "He didn't tell me that you got his daddy's job," she said bitingly, letting him know she was the one surprised not to have heard sooner.

Sean flashed a devilish grin. "I don't know," he teased. "Looks like Brian's the one who's got his daddy's job. Taking care of Evelyn. I think Carl would be proud to see his son at work." He tapped her toe with his boot.

"I think it would be better to continue this outside," Ruby said stiffly.

Sean hadn't stopped smiling. "You'd like to go outside to talk more about the way your son feeds a horse?"

"I'd like to get away from—" she started, and then changed her mind. "Yes, exactly," she continued sarcastically. "I'd like to go outside and hear if Brian holds the seed in his hand, or if he hangs up the whole bucket and leaves it at that. I want to know if he brushes Evelyn, too, and if he checks her hooves afterwards or not. Does he lift one of her front hooves first, or a back hoof? That's what I'd like to talk about outside." Ruby pointed one thumb over her shoulder to the door. "Right now."

"Or should we talk more about what I told him?" Sean asked, feigning sincerity.

"Come on," she directed, tilting her head toward the front of the room.

"Did he tell you that I said it's up to—"

"Outside," she commanded, linking an arm through his. She yanked him through the crowd. A chorus of oohs broke out in the bar as if he really had it coming. All eyes followed Sean and Ruby when they stormed, arm in arm, from the dark bar to the dim, smoky daylight outside. It was, unarguably, the most conspicuous exit Ruby had ever made.

Outside Bar 4, she found the smoky air refreshing. Sean faced her while she rested against the front door, relieved, as if she'd made an escape just in the nick of time. He leaned into her with one hand on the door, the other on his hip. The street was completely deserted.

"It felt a little crowded to you in there?" he asked, giving a laugh.

She glanced at his hand above her shoulder. "I don't always like an audience," she said.

"That's not what I hear," he said, fingering her neck, then returning his palm to the doorframe.

"We can't just do that," she said sternly. "Carl hasn't been gone three weeks, and I don't need the whole town listening to me invite you to live in my house." She was doing her best to keep her voice serious, concerned. But she felt him leaning into her, closing their space. Her words were coming out more and more slowly as she became aware of his focus on her eyes.

"Is that what you were doing?" he asked, playing dumb. His gaze was at once intense and vacant.

"You know that's what you were getting at," she said. Her words were ten times more assertive than her voice. "Of course Brian told me. And I don't know what you said to him, but he came back this morning grinning like an idiot." She faltered, realizing her choice of words described all too well what she was doing herself. "He came back grinning like an idiot," she couldn't believe she repeated, "with the idea that you move in. And I'm saying . . . I'm saying I agree. It makes sense. I'm saying why don't you come stay with us?"

Sean pretended to be confused. He dropped his hand from the door to her shoulder, this time keeping it there. "And you couldn't ask me that in there?" he said, lifting his chin toward the door. He leaned in closer as if that way he could better understand. His lips were almost to her ear. "What's so wrong with letting your brother-in-law come stay in your house while he's in town?" he asked. It was little more than a whisper.

She felt his breath wind through her ear as clearly as a

sip of ice water to her stomach on a hot, hot day. She took his jaw in her hand and pulled it firmly to her mouth. On the street, in the smoke, in the fuzzy light of day, she kissed him.

"I see," he said, staring at her, when she had pushed him away. But in the middle of the day, on Main Street, there was no one else who did.

Ruby wasn't sure about what she'd done. She wasn't sure if, when she'd kissed him, he had kissed her back. All she knew was that he hadn't tried to stop her. After she'd pushed his jaw from hers, Sean had lowered his hands to her hips and moved her away from the door. She'd heard a shout from the crowded room as he'd backed into Bar 4, and she'd watched his lips as he'd mouthed to her, "I'll see you." She had waited after the door closed behind him, to see if he wasn't actually going to return. When he didn't, she'd headed for her truck. If he *hadn't* really kissed her, she considered the whole way home, then she had done something she never should have done. If he hadn't really *wanted* her to kiss him, he might have gone inside and kissed one of those other women instead.

When Brian asked Ruby later that night if Sean was moving in, she spread both hands flat on the kitchen counter to steady herself. She barked at him that it wasn't any of his business, then apologized without lifting her eyes from the counter, and told him that she didn't know.

None of it should matter, she chided herself. So her kiss was out there with him, and no trace of him was here with her. So what? She lay on her back in bed, trying not to care, and drifted off into something short of sleep. Even with both windows open, there was no breeze—and so, fortunately, little smoke—but the air in the room grew stifling. Every few minutes she pushed at the top sheet until gradually it bunched around her feet. It twisted around her ankles like the chain of thought tangling her mind the more she tossed. Sean was probably at Bar 4 right now. She might have felt his lips take hers. Definitely nobody saw. No one could get in touch with Carl. If Sean wasn't at Bar 4, he was sleeping somewhere else. Maybe he *had* kissed one of them. But he had looked at her that *way.* Maybe his lips *had* held hers; she had no way of knowing. Maybe he *would* come to her house. She had no idea of the time.

Sean never did come to her house that night, and Ruby woke the next morning with the same thoughts playing through her head. It was the surest sign that something was bothering her if, upon waking, she found herself instantly

thinking of it, or him, or her. If she could get to the bathroom, brush her teeth, and go downstairs before dwelling
again on the concerns she'd fallen asleep with, then chances
were that whatever—or whoever—had been eating at her
wasn't so important after all. "If it's still there at daybreak,
it's something you can't shake," she always said. And Sean
was her first thought when she opened her eyes. As much as
she might have liked to, she couldn't deny that. Ruby
couldn't even roll over and read the clock to see how late
she'd slept before Sean was there in her head, along with
what she had done outside Bar 4.

Before she went to the bathroom, she crossed the hall to
check the guest room, in case Sean might have let himself in
through the unlocked front door during the night. Though
she had not expected to find him, she was disappointed to
see the guest room bed untouched, the pillows plump and
upright as if they, like Ruby, were anticipating someone's
arrival.

Brian's lesson in Marshall started at two o'clock that afternoon, and Ruby drove him, mostly in silence, to the Y. Although she sometimes stayed in Marshall during Brian's
lessons rather than making two round-trips to Whitticker,
today she wanted to keep driving. She could think more
clearly when she didn't stop moving, as if speed and motion
could prevent images of Carl in jail and Sean in Whitticker
from catching up with her. And what she was thinking, as
she drove home, was that she hoped to see Sean's truck in

her driveway when she returned. Or if not his truck in her driveway, then his bags unloaded in her front hall. Obviously, it would be tricky having him across the hall from her bedroom, but she could dismiss the matter for the time being. Because, for the time being, she didn't even know where he was. She had kissed her husband's brother, and she didn't know if he had kissed her back, and she didn't want him staying anywhere but her own house. That much she knew for certain.

But Sean's truck was not in her driveway when she arrived home. His bags were not in the front hall, nor at the top of the stairs, nor in the guest room, which she checked again as soon as she walked in. Ruby had an hour to wait before circling back to Marshall, and she sat on her front porch, facing town and listening to the distant rumbling of trucks, her nerves jumping at the thought that one might be coming her way. When, no more than twenty minutes later, the sound of a truck did come closer, Ruby rose to her feet. She cocked her ear toward the noise, and at the point where it might have turned and faded away, the rumble instead grew more distinct. For an instant, she imagined Sean carrying his belongings into her house and realized that perhaps this was something she should not have wished for. What had her mother said, when Ruby was a child, whenever she begged for something she could not have? Why on earth was she thinking of it now? Ruby craned her neck toward the truck's noise. She heard tires grab at the dirt as the truck forked off the paved road, and then it was in her sight, Sean's truck,

Sean's white truck with rust on the front fender and his duffel in the passenger seat, pulling up in front of her.

Before Sean cut the engine, Ruby was down off the porch on her tiptoes in the dirt. She smoothed one hand over the front of her shirt as Sean opened the truck's door. What was it her mother used to tell her? *Watch out what you ask for.* She couldn't remember exactly, but it had started something like that. *Someone might give you what you want.*

"Hey," Sean called, coming around the front of his truck, smiling. His face was sunburned and his hair slicked back as if he'd run his head under a faucet when he'd gotten off work.

"Hi," Ruby said, stepping forward to meet him. She lost track of whatever it was her mother used to say and reached a hand out to pat Sean's hip. "I was wondering if I'd see you," she said. She was always surprised by how composed she could sound even when she knew she was not.

Sean glanced at her hand. "Are you on your way out?" he asked. " 'Cause I can come back later if you are."

"No, no," she said quickly, also looking at her hand. She hadn't realized she'd been gripping the car keys in her fist since she got home. "I'm going to Marshall to get Brian, but not for a while." She slid the keys into her front pocket.

"Good," he said. "Because I just got off work, and . . . well . . . washing up at the ranch isn't so bad, but honestly, I've had enough of sleeping in my truck." He waited to see if she might pick up where he left off, or if he was going to have to be more explicit about why he'd come.

"Do you want help with your things?" Ruby asked abruptly, peering into his truck.

Sean was startled by her directness. "I thought about what you said yesterday," he started.

"Let's get your things," she said. She knew this would be easier to accomplish without a discussion.

Sean hesitated, his mouth open. "All right," he agreed slowly. He followed Ruby to the passenger door, which she had opened. "I wasn't sure if . . . You're sure that it's okay?" he asked.

Ruby was reaching for Sean's duffel in the front seat, but she stopped and straightened up to answer him. Sean had leaned in close behind her to lift the bag himself, and he had to take a quick step back to avoid colliding with her. They stood facing each other, inches apart, Sean pressing up against the open door, Ruby poised with one hand resting on the warm roof of the truck. Of course this wasn't *okay,* she almost said aloud. There was nothing *okay* about letting her husband's brother into her house—not given the trouble she was having keeping her hands to herself as they stood so close in the driveway. But the alternative was to let Sean go, and *that,* no matter what the consequence, was *not* going to happen.

"You're my brother-in-law," she said flatly, returning his own words from the day before.

He ran his eyes down the length of her body and up again. "I guess that's my point." He spoke seriously.

"No," Ruby sighed. She could smell he'd splashed on

aftershave as well as slicking back his hair. "That was *my* point yesterday. That's why I dragged you outside. So we wouldn't be in front of all those people." She stared at him willfully. "And you saw my point."

"Yeah, I did," Sean agreed softly.

"But you still came here," Ruby said, making him acknowledge she wasn't the only one whose intentions were questionable.

"Yeah." He smirked.

"So let's get your things." Ruby lowered her hand from the roof to Sean's duffel. She heaved the bag onto the dirt and lifted a second, smaller tote from the floor. "Come on," she said, carrying the tote up the porch steps, leaving the duffel for Sean.

Ruby stopped at the guest room threshold and waited for Sean to maneuver the long, fat duffel up the narrow staircase. She glanced at the guest room bed, its covers drawn tight across it, flawless as freshly fallen snow beckoning its first footprints. She felt her cheeks flush at the sight of it.

Sean dropped the duffel at the top of the stairs and joined her in the doorway. There was barely room for the two of them to face each other without touching. "In here?" He gestured toward the bed.

Ruby didn't raise her head. "Yeah," she said absently, entering the room sideways. "This is it." She went to the window first, ran her fingers along the sill, then sat down on the white bedspread.

Sean hauled the duffel through the door, and Ruby

checked her watch. She'd be early, but she could leave to get Brian anytime. Suddenly, she wanted to go. This was more than she had anticipated, the crisply made bed, the silent house, and Sean alone with her only a few feet away. It was what she had wanted, but for now she needed an out. Taking stock of the room, she couldn't believe how much she had overlooked when she'd cleaned up the day before. The silver-plated clock on the bureau was a Christmas gift from Carl. The bedside table lamp, that was a wedding present. In the closet, she remembered, was Carl's mother's wool blanket, as well as his heavy, quilted coat. They were details of her home she had stopped noticing years ago, but now they came hauntingly into focus, working at her conscience, shaking a finger at her for doing something wrong.

Sean sat down beside her on the bed, his leg against hers. "So," he started, patting her knee.

"So do you need anything for now?" Ruby asked, overriding further conversation as she stood up hastily. She pointed to her watch. "Because I need to pick up Brian." She was going to be earlier than she'd ever been before.

Sean smoothed the covers where Ruby's imprint remained. "No, I'm set," he said, surprised to hear she was leaving so soon. "I might just stay around the house and unpack." He stood up, hands on his hips. "If you don't mind."

"No, go ahead. Whatever you want," Ruby said, walking to the door. "I'll make dinner when I get back, so we can talk about . . . so we can talk more then."

"Actually, I think I'm going downtown later on," Sean said, cutting her short. "So don't worry about me for dinner." He swung the duffel up onto the bed, wrinkling the cover.

"Oh, okay," Ruby said, unable to hide the disappointment in her voice. She watched him unzip the duffel and part it wide open. In the top of the bag, she saw a worn leather pouch that she imagined held his toothbrush, his aftershave, those personal articles he would soon spread over the bathroom sink like an animal marking his territory. She paused in the doorway, confused that she could be both anxious to get out of the room and disappointed that he wouldn't be home when she returned.

"But I'll see you later," Sean confirmed.

"Yeah," she said from the top of the stairs. "See you later." She took a few steps down and then stopped, disturbed to be acting so awkwardly. With a deep breath, she collected herself and retraced her steps to the bedroom, poking her head in the door. "And hey," she said lightly then.

Sean looked up at her expectantly

"Welcome," she said, smiling this time, and waved a goodbye as she disappeared down the stairs.

Ruby didn't explain to Brian why she hardly spoke on the drive from Marshall to home. She knew he probably feared she was mad at him, and that he was likely racking his brain to find something he'd done wrong. But Ruby couldn't settle her own doubts long enough to put him at ease. Brian could handle a little discomfort, anyway, she figured, checking on him without turning her head. He looked so collected sitting beside her. *God,* she thought, noting the difference between her own recent behavior and his, *Brian could handle anything.*

"Where are we going?" he shrilled suddenly.

Ruby startled, dazed, as if he were waking her up.

Brian jutted his arm backward, and Ruby slammed on the brakes as the Whitticker exit disappeared behind them.

"Dammit," Ruby muttered under her breath as she pulled the truck onto the shoulder and shifted the gears into reverse. She reached one arm across the top of the seat and backed the truck up fast. "You didn't see your mom do that," she warned Brian. "Don't ever do that when you can drive." They were the first words out of her mouth since she'd picked him up.

Brian eyed Ruby suspiciously, expecting her to say more. "Is something going on?" he asked as they approached town.

Ruby was driving at barely a crawl, sitting forward almost at the windshield, scouring the main street. "No, Bri," she said, distracted. "There's nothing going on."

Brian hunched down, confused.

"But I do have some news," she added in a more lively voice.

"What?" Brian perked up.

"I talked to Sean," she announced. "And he's coming to stay with us. He brought his bags over this afternoon, and he's going to sleep in the guest room. Starting tonight."

"He's there right now?" Brian jumped in, sitting straight up with excitement.

"Well, he won't be there right now when we get home." Ruby prepared herself for that disappointment as much as she did Brian. "But all his things are there, and he'll be home later tonight. Maybe after you're in bed. And then he'll be around plenty."

"Ya-hooo," Brian howled, his chin high in the air. *"Sean's* staying at *our* house," he sang, bouncing up and down in his seat.

Brian's high voice rang in Ruby's head, where his words reverberated with far less innocence. She sat back in her seat, pressing harder on the gas, and asked him please to quiet down.

Ruby let Brian stay up later than usual because he wanted to see Sean. But hours after dinner, when Sean still hadn't returned, Ruby sent Brian to bed. By quarter after eleven, even she was getting tired of watching the clock. Besides, she didn't want Sean to think she'd been waiting for him, so she headed upstairs to her own bedroom.

At the top of the stairs, she hesitated in the empty hall. The lights were off in the guest room, but she peered into the darkness nonetheless. She sniffed the air and was pleased to discern a foreign scent in the room. She followed it across the threshold as if it were inviting her in, and she flicked on the light.

A pair of Sean's jeans was thrown across the bed. There

was a pile of loose change on the bedside table. Ruby studied this evidence of Sean without budging another inch inside the door. Even turning the lights on without him there seemed, to her, an improper invasion. Sure it was *her* room in *her* house, but with only a few of his belongings showing, it had been transformed to an unknown territory, every closed drawer a mystery.

The bedside table drawer was partway open. Ruby leaned into the hall to ensure she was alone, then tiptoed across the room to peek inside. The drawer was open just wide enough that she could see its contents without touching anything, and she held her hands behind her back, bent over with her nose only inches away. A few tattered matchbooks, each with a different New Mexico address, were strewn around a short stack of photographs. Ruby could see only the picture on top. In it, Sean sat at a picnic table with a man Ruby presumed was his father. Judging from Sean's bushier hair and slighter build, it was a picture taken many years ago. Ruby studied the plate of steaks in front of them, the shoulders of men on either side, the cans of beer littering the table, and tried to guess the occasion. It might have been a celebration, or a pack trip in the desert, or an ordinary night in someone's backyard. She was inclined to see it as a celebration because, with their arms around each other like that, with Sean's father holding a can of beer in the air, the two of them looked proud, like a team. Ruby examined his father's face—one she had never seen in person—and wondered if Carl would ever know that he had inherited his piercing eyes, his drawn and volatile gaze, from this man at the picnic table with his brother.

Ruby shut the drawer hard against the thought, and realized too late what she had done. When she opened it again, the matchbooks had slid to the back of the drawer, and the pictures had spilled from their neat pile. Now faces of women stared up at her: an air-brushed blonde wearing a red, tasseled vest; a dark-haired woman in a jean jacket, the name "Karla" scripted in gold on her lapel; a third woman, "Lilly," whose phone number was scrawled beneath her image. Ruby shoved the pictures into a pile, squaring the edges, and scattered the matchbooks again. Careful not to disturb the display, she inched the drawer into place and then hurried out of Sean's room to her own.

Ruby lay in bed trying to figure out what it was she wanted to say to Sean whenever he did arrive. Was she supposed to lay ground rules the minute he set foot in her house? Should she have said to him, right there in the driveway, there will be no funny business, you will sleep in your bed and I will sleep in mine? For God's sake, she'd already kissed him on the main street of Whitticker in the middle of the day. Her intentions might remain a secret to the rest of the town, but she couldn't pretend they were a secret to the two of them. Ruby thought she might ease her conscience by at least letting Sean know that she'd had misgivings, that she wasn't so brazen as to kiss her husband's brother without thinking twice. But she also wanted him to understand that she'd attracted plenty of men in the past without disrupting her own boundaries of marriage and motherhood. She'd handled this situation before, she wanted to tell him, and she could handle it now. Unless her desire was stronger this time. She wasn't sure. Ruby lay awake in the dark, trying to find the right words to say to Sean, but all she came up with were the ones she could never speak: *I won't admit I want you, but I refuse to let you go.*

10

Ruby wouldn't have guessed she could doze off before Sean came home, but she was asleep when he entered her room. The air in her bedroom was stagnant and hot, and she had tossed uncomfortably for hours. She was lying on her back with the top sheet cascading over the edge of the bed when the creak of a floorboard stirred her from sleep. Her T-shirt was pushed up to her chest and twisted from her restless turning, and she ran one hand along her bare thigh as she shifted her body and opened her eyes to see if there had, indeed, been a noise. A stream of moonlight filtered through the window across her body, but it seemed to her that the sun and morning couldn't be far away. She had no idea of the time. She heard another creak and, without moving her head, shifted her eyes from the window toward the door and saw Sean standing a few feet from her bed. Had she known for sure she wasn't dreaming, she would have been more startled to see him there. But as it was, in the opalescent light of the room, his presence seemed no more than a confirmation that he must have been thinking about her, too, wherever he had been that evening. Sean seemed to be waiting to see if he had woken her, but when he advanced into the line of moonlight where she could make out his eyes, he didn't appear fazed to see that she was watching him. He didn't say a word, but he appeared to have come with a purpose. Ruby didn't say a word either as Sean stepped to her side so that his knees nudged the bed. He froze there, towering above her, and Ruby considered that he might have made a wrong turn at the top of the stairs and come into her room, disoriented, by accident. She was about to reach for the sheet to cover herself when Sean leaned forward. But where she anticipated he would come down toward her face, he bent over her smooth, bare belly instead. He placed his palms on the mattress, one at her hips and one at her chest, and he brought his lips to her skin, and he kissed her.

Ruby didn't move under Sean's bent figure, and even if she'd found what she wanted to say, she didn't have the voice. Sean was the one who had figured out what to say without speaking a word. The time she'd spent deliberating in the car and in bed seemed unnecessary to her now; in one, swift gesture Sean demonstrated what she feared it was not possible to express. And as he straightened up and pinned his eyes to hers, he also let her know that, yes, whether or not he should have, a part of him had claimed her.

As he turned to leave, the floorboards sounded Sean's exit. The creaking confirmed to Ruby their encounter had been real, and she raised her head from the pillow to get her bearings. Through her half-open door she could see across the hall to the light in Sean's bedroom. She saw his jacket thrown over the bed, one sleeve dangling almost to the floor. She watched him slip out of her room, closing the door behind him, and but for a sliver of white across the floor, the light from his room disappeared. She lay motionless as if he were still there above her. She wondered how long he had been home. It could have been any time, the middle of the night or the beginning of the day. She didn't care either way. Sean was across the hall, and he'd shown her that he wasn't going anywhere else. And in that instant, in her best instinct, it felt like the beginning.

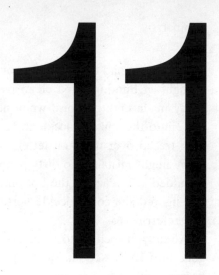

S ean's truck stalled as he was pulling out of the Flying
C three days later, and he almost changed his mind
about going to the Whitticker Inn. He took the key out of
the ignition, threw it down on the dashboard, and reached
for the sandwich he'd made in Ruby's kitchen that morning.
It was bologna with mayonnaise on white bread, a combination that reminded him he was sharing a house with an
eight-year-old. Sean had used the last of the bologna, and
he'd written Ruby a note on the greasy white deli wrapping,
telling her he would bring home more. It was their first com-
munication since Sean closed her door in the middle of the

night, and he had deliberated about what to write. First he'd
thought of hunting for a clean piece of paper, but he'd already made enough noise when he'd dropped the sandwich
knife into the sink by accident. He wrote the note in pencil,
then traced over the faint letters with a pen, concerned that
Ruby might mistake the dirty paper for garbage. Impulsively
he added a P.S. across the bottom, *P.S. Did I wake you up?*,
and figured she could decide herself which early morning he
was referring to.

Already, it seemed to Sean more than two days since he'd
gone into Ruby's room. Between leaving for work early and
hanging out at Bar 4 late, he had been in her house only in
the hours she was asleep or at work or in Marshall with
Brian. At night, lying in bed, he could hear her deep, steady
breathing across the hall. By day, the recollection distracted
him from his work. Sean wasted hours wondering what Ruby
must be thinking of him for appearing in her room. At the
time, he hadn't thought twice about going to her bedside—
only that he saw something he wanted, and that perhaps she
had left her door half open so he would see. But now, Sean
was avoiding the sight of her again. He couldn't remember
the last time he'd felt like this—if he had *ever* felt like this—
like a school boy whose palms grew sweaty at the mention
of his secret love's name.

He hurriedly finished eating his sandwich and checked his
watch to see how much time he had to make up his mind.
It was five past noon, and Sean watched through his windshield as the other wranglers gathered by the office and

headed off together for lunch. Every Friday, Mitch and Lyle and the rest of them took an extended lunch break in town for heaping plates of burgers and fries and slaw. But Sean had told them he had an errand to take care of and wouldn't be joining them. If he went right away, he'd have a good hour with Ruby before she left for Marshall with Brian. Except that now his truck had stalled, and minutes were passing, and he wasn't sure it had been the best idea in the first place. His truck had also stalled in Ruby's driveway the past two mornings, but rather than dismiss its sputter and cough as a nuisance this time, Sean took it as a sign that perhaps he should exercise better judgment than to drive to the Whitticker Inn Trading Post and surprise Ruby.

He squeezed the sandwich's plastic wrap into a tight ball in his fist.

"Sean." One of the younger wranglers, Sam Ferguson, jogged up from behind the truck to its open window. "You coming?" he asked, pointing to the men heading away in a pack.

"No, no," Sean said purposefully. "I've got a thing to take care of. I've got to get going." He took the keys from the dashboard before Sam could ask more questions, and this time the engine started smoothly.

The Whitticker Inn was an old, wooden building at the opposite end of Main Street from the Early Bird and Bar 4. Its original entrance—the double oak doors with lavender stained glass in the windowpanes and ornate coach lamps fixed to either side—had been restored several times since the inn first opened in the twenties, and after two expansions over its seventy-odd years, the rambling hotel occupied most of the block. A wide, shaded porch ran along the front with a swinging settee at each end adorned with flowered pillows. Uneven dips in the wooden front steps dated back to the years when the inn had seen a steady flow of visitors. In recent years, however, business had been increasingly slow, especially in the summer months, when the brutal heat virtually shut the place down. With the fires now and all the smoke, Sean wouldn't have been surprised to hear there was not a single guest in the Whitticker Inn.

But the Trading Post off the front lobby drew customers, if not in droves, at least in a steady trickle throughout the year. A sign outside the building hailed the post's selection of native turquoise jewelry in bolder letters than it advertised the inn's vacancy, cable TV, and biscuit breakfast. Ruby had worked at the Trading Post since high school, when her mother used to work there, too. She suspected her mother and the inn's owner, Leonard Cranshaw, had been having an affair most of the time her mother was employed there. She speculated that her stepfather's decision to move the three of them across the state was motivated by her mother's suspiciously long hours at the Trading Post. But Ruby had chosen to stay in town with Carl when her parents left Whitticker. And though Carl had insisted she quit her job and let him provide for their family, Ruby had continued working three half-days a week, dusting kachina dolls and arranging chunky turquoise jewelry inside the vast glass cases lining the perimeter of the store.

Sean parked behind the inn and took his time walking around to the front. There was no one at the reception desk when he entered the lobby, but he imagined that the jangling bells on the door would bring someone, perhaps the owner himself, to the front momentarily. To avoid encountering anyone other than Ruby, Sean quickened his pace. He rushed across the patterned carpet toward a life-size wooden Indian chief guarding the Trading Post's open door. The doorframe was fashioned of rustic pine logs that distinguished the shop from the finer lace and scarlet trimmings of the inn itself. Sean's boots smacked against the store's wide wooden floorboards in startling contrast to his hushed strides along the carpet.

Ruby rose up from behind a glass case at the sound of Sean's entrance. Her strawberry hair was down straight, tucked behind her ears, and she wore a light denim button-down shirt with her blue jeans. At the sight of Sean, she tumbled several turquoise rings to the counter, clattering their chunky rocks against the glass, dropping one over the case to the floor.

"Hey, stranger," Sean said brightly, crossing the room and picking up the ring at his feet. It was a relief to see her again, in daylight, where she appeared more approachable than the image that had inflated in his mind.

Ruby smiled curiously, her interest piqued that, for a second time now, Sean had come to her unannounced. "That was my line, stranger," she said, holding out her palm. "Where've you been?"

Sean dropped the polished hunk into her hand. "Working," he said dismissively. "Playing." He surveyed the wood-paneled room, surreptitiously checking his watch as he did. "So this is the place."

"Working and playing," Ruby repeated, as if she were not convinced by his answer.

"Yeah," Sean said, fingering the other rings on the counter. "And you?"

"I've been wondering if there's anyone sleeping across the hall from me," she said flippantly, disappearing behind the case to slide a glass door shut. "I've been wondering if I was dreaming."

Sean could see only the top of her head below the counter. He hadn't expected her to be so confrontational, at least not so soon after he'd walked in. "No," he said feebly, clearing his throat.

Ruby stood up. "No?" she questioned forcefully, pretending not to have heard, challenging him to say it again.

Sean spread his hands on the counter. "You were not," he said clearly, looking at his hands, careful not to look at her. He strummed his fingers once against the glass, physically drumming his confession away. "Do you want to have lunch?" he asked then, his voice stronger. He wasn't going to let her make him forget why he'd come.

"Lunch?" she repeated.

Sean heard the foolishness of his proposition in the tone

with which Ruby shot it back at him. Of course, she was right; he was kidding no one to suggest he'd be satisfied sitting across from her in a booth, with a ketchup bottle and a napkin dispenser and paper place mats between them. Neither of them wanted another public display. But Sean continued casually. "I have some time," he said, "and since we haven't been seeing each other, I thought I'd come by and check if you'd be able to get off long enough for a sandwich."

Ruby thought of the note she'd found on the deli wrapping and sharpened her eyes on Sean knowingly. "Right now?"

"It *is* lunch time," Sean said, turning the face of his watch toward her.

And you have all my bologna, she wanted to say, but she held her tongue. "Let me see." She thumbed through a notebook by the cash register, then checked her own watch. "Sure," she said, drawing the word out slowly, exploring this opportunity in her mind. "I can probably close up an hour early. I'll leave a note for the afternoon girl." She tore a piece of paper from the notebook. "This place has been dead anyway."

"The smoke is still pretty bad," Sean said. "There aren't many people out."

"Summers are always slow." She turned a key in the register and walked around to Sean's side of the counter. "Come with me," she directed him. "I have to grab my bag."

In the lobby, Ruby eyed the front door and the sweeping

staircase to the guest rooms before she ducked behind the reception desk. Sean heard a jingle from the desk, but when Ruby stood up, she did not have her bag.

"Follow me," she said. She crossed the lobby briskly and started up the stairs. "I should make sure there's no one around who's gonna mind if I close up." She waved Sean up the stairs.

He hesitated with one hand on the sturdy, round newel post, surprised that she would care to be so thorough.

"You never know with old Lenny," she said as if she could hear Sean thinking.

At the top of the first flight of stairs, Ruby halted and held her hand out for Sean to halt, too. "Nope," she said, checking the narrow hall in both directions. "I don't see anyone."

Sean followed a few paces behind, telling himself to control his imagination, that Ruby wasn't leading anywhere except a staff room where she kept her bag. But he knew she wouldn't go out of her way like this to find someone who would then witness them together in those empty halls. He knew something was suspicious.

They had turned left toward another stretch of rooms when Ruby again held out her hand like a stop sign. He watched her peer down the corridor, her chin raised, alert, and he felt more confident of his suspicions, that she was sniffing for danger.

"Nope," she said after her brief inspection. "I guess there's no one around." She started down the second long corridor on the balls of her feet and stopped at a door near the end, where the number twenty-seven was etched into a gold plate in simple black lines. She drew a key out of her front pocket, unlocked the door, and swung it open into a modest bedroom filled mostly by a queen-size bed.

"Nope," she said a third time, stepping into the room. "Looks like it's not going to be a problem if I close up. I just wanted to make sure that everything was set."

This time it was Sean who was taken by surprise. He remained rooted to the threshold, his eyes roving across the bed, the wooden writing desk, the lamps with lace-trimmed shades and doilies at their base, delicate gold pull chains dangling from the bulbs. Ruby did not turn the lights on. She maneuvered around Sean in the narrow entranceway and shut the door. She rotated the lock on the knob, then slid the gold chain into place. When she turned around, Sean was right there behind her.

A yellowed shade was drawn over the only window at the far end of the room, and thin lines of daylight filtered around its edges, across the carpet, to their ankles. The sterile smell of disinfectant, of a place where the carpet would always have vacuum tracks and the toilet paper was folded daily into a triangle, filled the room. Sean and Ruby didn't need to speak to agree that the anonymity of such a place granted them a freedom almost frightening.

"But I'm afraid there's no room service," Ruby started coyly.

"I've got everything I need," Sean whispered before she

could finish, and instinctively he took hold of her hips. He pulled her to him, and she raised her hands to his shoulders and pushed him firmly toward the bed. They fell back on the mattress and tossed their blue jeans in a tangle to the floor. They moved their bodies deftly over each other as if they'd been exchanging thoughts for days, though the truth was that, for the first time since Sean had pulled into town, both he and Ruby had, finally, stopped thinking. And though they dared not spend more than thirty minutes absent from the world outside, it was long enough, in the dim light of the room, for the two of them to discover a place where such things as chores with horses and trips to Marshall did not apply. Protected by the hotel room walls, they felt this new space was one they could leave behind and return to as they wanted.

Afterward, they lay side by side on their backs, legs overlapping, and stared up to the ceiling. They'd stayed on top of the covers so as not to mess the sheets, but the bedspread was twisted and bumpy. Sean turned, facing Ruby, and lifted her torso so he could straighten the bedspread beneath her.

"There," he said when he lowered her back down. He propped himself up on his elbow and spread his free hand over her stomach. He fanned his fingers out and back and noted the contrast of his tanned, callused hand against her pale skin.

She wriggled beneath his ticklish strokes.

"You still need lunch," he said, breaking the silence.

Ruby smiled, but didn't turn her eyes to his. She gazed

distantly at the ceiling, savoring her last moments away from life outside that hotel room door. *"Hmmm,"* she hummed, weighing her options, and she rested her hand over Sean's hand on her stomach. She squinted as if a menu might be written in fine print on the ceiling, but her expression indicated considerations more serious.

"I want a piece of pie," she said after a long silence.

Sean laughed, running his hand from her stomach to her chin and tilting her head toward him. "Pie?" he questioned.

Ruby shifted onto her side to face him. "Pie. From the Early Bird," she said, matter of fact. "But I guess I can't go there now," she sighed, and glanced at her wrinkled clothes on the floor. "After this."

Sean wasn't sure if she was serious. She had led him to this room and locked the door, and now, lying beside him naked, she was thinking about pie? "What kind of pie?" he asked, amused.

"Strawberry," Ruby said automatically. "With whipped cream from a can. But it doesn't really matter. I just want a piece of pie."

Sean's mouth hung open as he contemplated her request. "Okay," he said dubiously. "If that's what you want, then I suppose we can go—" And then he stopped himself short. "But wait a minute," he said, turning his palm faceup on her stomach. "Why pie?"

Ruby rolled toward him, and his palm slid across her ribs to the small of her back. "Because think of when you eat it," she said.

"Ruby, I don't remember the last time I ate a—"

"Because you don't eat it every day." She sat up as if he'd proved her point exactly as she'd wanted. "But then think about those other times. I think back to when I'm ten years old and my mom makes a pie on my birthday, or it's Thanksgiving and there's a big table of us at my grandparents', or Brian gets good grades and I bake for him, or I'm in the market and I'm sick of this town and my life and I say screw it, I'm buying a pie for myself, and I'll eat it right out of the box with a plastic fork from the deli counter."

She paused to see if Sean was listening, and she was pleased to see him marveling at her.

"And then the next morning when you wake up," she continued, "when you go downstairs, there's the leftover pie on the counter. You peel back the plastic wrap, and you have pie for breakfast, right at the counter without sitting down, like you're sneaking something. Just because it's there. And it's only there in the first place because it marks something—either something is different, or special, or maybe even really bad. But there's always a reason when you eat pie. It's never for nothing."

She stopped talking then, and Sean looked at her quizzically. He would have thought her explanation ridiculous except that with it she smoothed away any awkwardness between them more masterfully than he could have done himself. He had driven to the inn nervous as an eight-year-old, and now he felt—he thought they both felt—as though he belonged there.

"Well, we don't have to go to the Early Bird," he suggested. "We can go to . . . I don't know." He stumbled, trying to think of other places. "We can go to . . . to *anywhere* for a piece of pie."

Ruby climbed on top of him playfully, her eyes lit up. "Okay," she said, fitting her hands under his back. "Take me to anywhere for a piece of pie. Strawberry if they've got it. *That,*" she said, squeezing him to her, "sounds like a plan."

She slid off Sean and knelt to the floor to retrieve her clothes. She tossed Sean's jeans to him and tugged her own over her hips. Once he was up, Ruby smoothed the bedspread, and Sean ran his hands over their footprints in the carpet as if wiping steam from a window. Without speaking, they returned the room to its untouched state, removing traces of themselves with increasing speed as they grew anxious to complete their transition, to get Sean back to work unquestioned, Ruby on her way to Marshall like so many other afternoons.

They stood in the cramped entranceway, assessing the room one last time.

"Okay?" Sean asked, to see if Ruby was ready to make a break out of the door.

"Okay," she confirmed, businesslike, mustering the courage to reach for the knob. "We're off to anywhere for a piece of pie," she chimed with forced levity, checking over her shoulder for Sean's reaction.

"I actually have to get back to work," he said regretfully, raising his watch.

"I know." She shrugged her shoulders, deflated. "And I have to take Brian to Marshall."

"But it's a good thought." Sean smiled. "I'd rather go to anywhere than to work."

"To where they always have pie." Ruby reached her hand to the door.

"Some other day," Sean inhaled, anticipating the turn of her wrist on the knob.

"I'll hold you to it," she murmured, and leaned sideways into him.

They hurried down the hall in silence, briskly descending the stairs to the lobby. At the entrance to the Trading Post, Ruby waved Sean to go ahead of her toward the front door.

"You go first," she whispered.

"You wait here five minutes," he said.

Sean breezed across the lobby and out the double doors. He jogged to his truck and drove straight to the Early Bird. In the raised glass case behind the counter lay a fresh strawberry pie with one piece cut out. But as Sean flagged a waitress to take his order, he thought better than to ask for Ruby's favorite dish. He changed his request in the nick of time, so that when he swung his truck in front of the Whitticker Inn minutes later, it was a piece of peach pie, not strawberry, that he handed to Ruby through his open window. Peach pie, smothered in whipped cream from the can.

12

I n the Keyanta Men's Correctional Facility, in a six-by-nine cell, Carl couldn't believe his luck: his release might soon be negotiated with no more than the tweaking of a few details. He kept his fingers crossed. There was no better way to pass the empty, unmarked days, he figured, than to think of when they'd be behind him. He didn't need any tally on his walls to remind him he was already at the start of his twenty-second day. It wasn't a count he was going to lose track of. Especially now that his court-appointed lawyer had recommended he change his plea to guilty. If the lawyer was for real, Carl was thinking—if changing his plea and tailoring the events of that disastrous day could really turn a potential four-year sentence into probation—then he needn't hesitate at all. Then he might have only a few weeks left, and so what if he couldn't go back to Whitticker telling everyone he wasn't guilty? Too many of them had been right there to see him lose his mind. Serving time couldn't change that. And anything would be better than looking at these four gray walls another day. He laughed out loud to think how he would welcome a pink elephant on the wall. Any splash of color, any sign of life. Even his standard-issue jumpsuit wasn't orange or blue like the ones he'd seen on TV. Even it was a lifeless gray.

Though he'd already done it too many times over, Carl counted the forty-three spidery cracks on the ceiling again. They ran into each other like the nights and mornings when he lay on his back or stood in the center of the cell with his arms out, palms pushing flat and hard against either wall, regretting what this confinement had cost him. More than he might have guessed, he missed Ruby and Brian and Max, on the front porch, in the fresh air, at home. At least he still got to feel the fresh air every day, he consoled himself. At one o'clock, after lunch, a mechanical bell would grant permission for him and the other thirty-nine men in his cluster to see the sky for forty minutes from the southeast cement courtyard. It was a cruel taste of the most fundamental part of his old life, but at least he wasn't forgetting the touch of soft air on his skin. As for Ruby and Brian, he wasn't sure when he would touch either of them again.

That was the question that increasingly confused him. Because Carl knew that when all of this started three weeks earlier, his intention had been never to touch Ruby again. But as he approached a month now, of blurred days and timed air and lukewarm, pasty meals, the intention was as much as he could remember for sure. And even *that* he remembered clearly only because it had landed him in jail. Otherwise, memories washed through his head without any dates or definition. He knew he had been furious with Ruby; he knew, more than that, he had been in love. He knew he had tried to leave her; he didn't know any longer, exactly, why.

He conceded that thoughts like these were bound to happen in a place where the focus was on time passing. Only the hours came and went. Only the sun changed position. Even after years of wasting time, of blowing afternoons on beer and bad TV, Carl had never felt quite so stuck, absolutely motionless, while the world, on the other side of the compound walls, moved on without him. Never by force before had he stayed so still. It was threatening to drive him nuts. And yet, he realized, if he hadn't lost his freedom, he'd probably be doing equally little back at home. But that was assuming that if he were not in jail, he *would* be back at home. And three weeks earlier, that hadn't been the plan. If all had gone well when he'd run out of the store with the money in his hand, he'd have been far from Whitticker by now. As it was, with all of the empty time and gray space, he couldn't tell if he still wanted that kind of freedom. He didn't know if it was freedom he wanted, or simply to get back home.

Sitting on the edge of his mattress, with his knuckles at his temples and his eyes on the floor, Carl tried to recall what had been so bad about Ruby. He was angry he couldn't remember. He could picture only her wide smile, her fiery hair. He could see her sunburned face at seventeen. It would have been easier if he could remember instead the reasons behind his beers and insults and plans to leave. He wasn't kidding himself that she'd never thrown her eyes at half of Whitticker; but alone in his cell, all of that seemed much less important than the fact that she had once been his. Carl let the old, good memories expand inside him. They colored his cell and helped him to pass the afternoon.

After dinner, after a long day of thinking back, Carl decided to take the guards up on an offer they'd made him a few days earlier. Now he wanted to make a phone call after all. Normally, inmates were granted supervised calls on a regular basis, but because Carl had raised a fist at the first guard who suggested he use the phone the day after he arrived, further calls had been withdrawn indefinitely. Carl didn't care about his phone privileges either way; he wished he'd gone ahead and given that guard his best slug for needling him to call his wife and family like a responsible man. *Like that pink-skinned kid knew what it was to have a wife and son,* Carl grimaced.

When the guards had offered Carl another chance to make

a call, he'd brushed them off hostilely. He told them not to worry, he wasn't taking any of their favors. But now he lay in bed mulling over what his lawyer had told him: if he changed his not-guilty plea to guilty, he might not be sentenced at all. Carl sometimes forgot he wasn't even working off a sentence yet. He was still waiting to be tried. His lawyer told him that for such a small case, a trial would be fast and careless, and a not-guilty plea would most likely keep him in jail. But switch to guilty, play up the facts—the gun wasn't loaded, no one was hurt, Carl had been distraught, maybe even mentally abused, and drunk—and he might walk out of Keyanta close to free. At least that's what five years' probation sounded like to Carl from the inside of his cell. And best of all, the whole bargaining process could take place, if done with cooperation—the lawyer had nudged him—within a few weeks. The state of Arizona didn't need to get bogged down with every drunk cowboy who raised his own little bit of hell, he'd told Carl as he snapped his briefcase closed. To Carl, it all sounded too good, too fast, too easy, to be true. But at the same time, he felt he might have one foot pretty close to stepping out the door.

So he changed his mind and told the guards he wanted to make that call. It was his twenty-second night, just after dinner, and he figured Ruby would be home. He wanted to tell the Ruby he'd been holding in his mind all day that in a few more weeks he might be home. He wanted her to hear the Carl she'd kissed in the janitor's closet at Wood River High and to tell him she'd be waiting. He turned his back to the guard and dialed his own home number with a trembling finger. On the third ring, Brian answered, and Carl almost hung up. It took him a second to realize he hadn't dialed the wrong number.

"Hello?" Brian repeated. Carl hadn't given a thought to his son as he'd prepared to make the call. He'd only imagined how Ruby would sound. "I'm going to hang up," Brian said, almost politely.

Carl felt his stomach lurch. This hadn't crossed his mind. He was upset with himself for being disappointed. He was upset that Brian sounded so far away.

"Hi, Bri," he said slowly, and his voice cracked with uncertainty. He thought it might have been better to hang up. Certainly, it would have been easier.

"Dad!" Brian shouted immediately. His high voice sprung from the receiver. From two hundred miles away, it disarmed Carl. "Where are you, Dad?" Brian shouted, his voice shrill with excitement.

With one hand to his mouth, Carl realized he hadn't smiled this way in too long to remember. He touched his lips where they curled up into his cheeks. "I'm way up in the corner of the state, Bri," he said almost as if it were good news. "I'm about six hours away."

"What are you *doing?*" Brian asked in a shaky voice, moving his knees back and forth as if he were running in place. He could hardly contain himself. It was his *dad* on the phone. He couldn't think what to say.

"I'm doing my best to get out of here, Bri," Carl said.

"I'm doing everything I can to get back home." Hearing his own voice say it gave Carl greater conviction that soon it would be true. He felt it was the right thing to say to Brian. From so far away, he believed it was the best he could do.

His words sent Brian spinning. "When are you coming home?" he yelled into the phone. He stopped shaking his knees and leapt once into the air.

"What was that?" Carl asked, avoiding the question when he heard Brian's feet thud onto the floor.

"I jumped up," Brian said. "Will you be home for my swim meet? It's in sixteen days. I'm in four races."

Carl didn't think he should reveal too much more. "Well, I can't say for sure," he said, choosing his words carefully. "But I'm working on it, and I wanted to talk to your mom for a minute." He said it as if the two were logically related. "Can you get her for me?" He didn't hear how curt it sounded.

Brian hesitated. "She's not here," he said quietly, hurt that his dad would make their conversation so short. He'd wanted to tell him more about his races. "She's out with Sean," he said. "Putting gas in the truck and going for a quick drive, and then they'll be right back." His words fell flat and hard between them.

"With Sean?" Carl repeated after a long pause. He'd long since written off the chance that his brother might actually help him. "Sean came for Evelyn?" He couldn't imagine it.

"He came to get her," Brian said, "but he's waiting for

when the foal is born. He wants to see if Evelyn will be okay for a trip."

Carl remained quiet, silenced by the possibilities he hadn't considered when he'd called Sean. He didn't like how it sounded when Brian said that: *She's out with Sean.* It made Carl uneasy to speculate why his brother was doing him a favor he'd sworn never to do.

"Sean said how you were a hero when Evelyn was born," Brian offered, to break the silence. It was something he'd been looking forward to telling his father someday anyway. "He said how everyone thought so."

"Did he," Carl said flatly. He didn't want to hear that Sean was telling his son stories. All he'd wanted when he'd made that phone call to Sean was a favor. Otherwise, he didn't want his brother back in his life at all.

"Yeah," Brian said timidly, confused by the change in his father's voice. "He said how they all cheered you." He coughed to try to get rid of the lump in his throat.

Carl pressed his fists against the wall, turning his knuckles white. "Well, don't listen to everything your uncle tells you," he said sharply.

Brian didn't know if that meant his father wasn't a hero after all. "Is something wrong, Dad?" he asked.

"Yeah, Bri, I'm in jail," Carl snapped bitterly before he could stop himself. *I'm in jail, and my brother is living with you,* he might as well have said. The ugly silence that followed stung them both. Brian was growing dizzy in the center of the kitchen, where he stood with his knees now locked.

He tasted the salt in tears running to his mouth. More than anything, he was terrified his father would hang up.

"Sorry," he choked, though he didn't know what he'd done wrong.

"No, no, no," Carl retorted. He pounded his fist against the wall. "Don't you say that, Bri. This is *my* fault." He stopped short, surprised to hear himself admit it. "This is something *I've* done," he explained, talking fast, "and you need to go wipe your face before your mother gets home because this is going to be okay. Do you hear me?" He heard a sniffle on the other end. "You gotta tell me that you hear me, Bri," he said again. "Because this is all going to end up fine. I swear."

Brian was frozen in place. "Are you going to come home?" he asked, his voice a squeaky whisper.

"I'm doing my best," Carl said. "You tell your mom that."

"Okay," Brian said. He wiped his cheek on his shirtsleeve.

"Okay," Carl said, as if he were confirming something. He didn't know what more to offer. He wasn't sure how he should say good-bye. "Hey," he said instead, giving them a little more time. "Tell me a story about home before I have to hang up."

Brian looked around the room, trying to find something to tell him. *"Umm,"* he said while he looked. His eyes settled on the open window, where a thin thread of smoke wafted in. "The fires will be over soon," he said. "They were really big this time—I think the biggest ever, but Mom doesn't know. Probably in a week they'll be gone. I don't know."

"Really," Carl said. "Was the smoke bad?"

"Yeah, it was really bad," Brian said, nodding his head. "It was so bad that one day I didn't even go outside—"

"No kidding." Carl broke in, impressed. He was relieved to hear his son's voice grow stronger again.

"Yeah, and we closed all the windows, and I opened the refrigerator door on me, and Mom pretended to close me in, it was so hot."

"Wow," Carl said, dramatically. "That's something."

"Yeah," Brian agreed, beginning to move his knees back and forth again. "But they're mostly gone now. In a week, they'll be over."

"That'll be good," Carl said, checking over his shoulder to the guard. He felt better about saying good-bye now that Brian sounded happy. "But you know what, Bri, I have to get going now, because where I am you're not allowed to talk and talk and talk."

Brian tried to imagine where that place was, then stopped himself. "Okay," he said. He held his knees together and looked at the ground.

"So you be good," he said.

"I am," Brian said right away.

Carl laughed. "I know you are," he said. Even if it wouldn't last long for either of them, he wanted to picture that Brian was smiling, too. "Okay, Bri," he said, "I gotta go now."

"Okay, Dad," he said.

"I'll see you."

"Bye."

Brian listened for the dial tone before he hung up.

Carl walked rapidly ahead of the guard to his cell. He stretched his neck back and rolled his head along his shoulders to ward off the sadness that threatened him. In his cell, he stood with his palms out flat on either wall and concentrated on the one part of their conversation that didn't hurt: the fires. In a week, he heard Brian's sweet, high voice telling him, they'd be over for sure. Then the mountain would be black and the air would be clear, and the sky would be open again. In his cell, in the dark, Carl tried to guess where he might be by then. In a week, when the fires had ended, he might be anywhere.

13

Ruby was waiting in Sean's truck in the alley behind the Early Bird, wondering what was taking him so long. She slumped down in her seat with her knees up against the dashboard, keeping an eye on the rearview mirror in case someone other than Sean should come along. Not that sitting in his truck was suspicious behavior; there were myriad reasons why she might be with him—running errands or picking up food—in the middle of the week on their lunch breaks. But Ruby had hardly run her fingers through her tousled hair as they'd left room 27 twenty minutes earlier, and when she bowed her head to her chest and pressed her nose against the inside of her shirt collar, she smelled Sean's scent, not her own, on her skin. He'd been in the Early Bird at least ten minutes already, and they both needed to get back to work.

Sean and Ruby had been taking longer lunch breaks in the week since their first secret meeting, as if their initial success were enough to justify forming a casual habit out of a dramatic risk. Ruby had even agreed to drive with Sean to the Early Bird after they'd systematically tidied the room, though she stayed in the truck while he went inside. So far, she'd never seen anyone else in the alley while she waited. But those few minutes of anticipating Sean's return always quickened her pulse, and now she pondered what exactly the logic might be behind her growing simultaneously more cavalier and more nervous about their conduct. Ruby checked her watch and tapped her fingers against her thighs. *What,* she wondered as she visualized the waitress lifting the pie from the case, slicing a piece, placing it in a Styrofoam box shaped for a hamburger, *could take so long?*

Finally Sean appeared in the rearview mirror, taking hurried strides and carrying a brown bag in his hand. He swung open his door and handed the bag to Ruby as he climbed inside.

"What took you so long?" she demanded anxiously, sitting up again. The smell of grease and fried onions rushed into the truck with him like a blast of hot air.

"I didn't think I was going to get out of there," he groaned. "That old guy from the saddlery . . . I can't remember his name. I've met him with Lyle once. Gray hair, scar on his chin. He was in there in line, and he started talking to me, asking how I'm finding things in town, how the job is, all of this." Sean rolled his eyes. "He says he's got some niece visiting or something, that I should meet her, that she's *some* drink of water. I kept heading for the door, but he was going on and on." Sean took Ruby's wrist and looked at her watch. "Jesus," he said, reaching for the ignition.

"So what did you tell him?" she asked, smirking but interested. She spread her hand over the inside of his thigh.

"That I'm sleeping with my brother's wife, but thanks anyway." Sean turned the engine over and shot Ruby a smile.

"Shut up." She laughed tensely. "Not funny," she said to the beat of two hard smacks against his leg.

"He took it well," Sean teased, then cleared the grin from his face. "But I should go," he said. "I've *got* to go. Do you want me to pick up Brian?"

Brian had gone to a friend's house across town for the day.

"Thanks," Ruby said. "But I should probably get him myself."

"Okay," Sean said, shrugging. He ran his hand over her thigh and squeezed her knee. "See you later, then."

Ruby cast a quick glance in the rearview mirror before she leaned over and kissed him, something neither of them had done in the alley behind the Early Bird before.

"Whoa," Sean exclaimed when she slid away from him. "You're bolder than I," he said, as she hopped out the door.

Ruby liked the sound of his admission, and spontaneously

she placed the brown bag on the truck's roof and made another covert check up and down the deserted alley. Then she took the bottom of her shirt in her hands and raised it in a quick flash up to her chin. Her white bra, her milky skin, filled Sean's view through the side window. He whistled his approval as he gave the truck's horn two long honks, and Ruby frantically yanked her shirt down and gaped at him, glowing but shocked.

"Two can play," Sean said, leaning across to the open window and winking at her. "You better get to work."

Ruby snatched the bag from the roof and spun away from Sean, jogging down the alley lightly and carelessly at first. With the pie in her hand and one more easy hour of work ahead before she'd pick up Brian and drive home to Sean, Ruby thought her life might never have been this complete. But as she put more distance between herself and Sean, her strides grew heavier. Plodding past an overturned garbage can, she wondered what the hell the two of them were thinking, behaving like this, practically asking to get caught. By the time she rounded the corner onto Main Street, her feet dragged one after the other as if she were lugging chunks of the sidewalk along with her. She pictured Sean returning to the Flying C and wondered if he felt the same weight slowing him down.

It was ridiculous that her mood could fall so quickly, in the course of just a few blocks, but by the time Ruby reached the inn, she thought she might cry over her own selfishness, over the possibility that she couldn't handle getting away with whatever she wanted. The brown paper bag she carried hid the pie like a secret about to explode. Not two minutes earlier her happiness had seemed unshakable. But outside the double doors, bending over to catch her breath, Ruby choked on a gulp of air laced with smoke and was relieved to have an alternative to sobbing. She heaved open the inn's door and walked across the lobby with her hand in the air, waving her way through the insidious smoke as if she'd walked into a low cobweb blindly.

The last of the firefighters left town one week later. Ruby was standing in the hall between her room and Sean's that morning, wearing the undershirt Sean had taken off when they'd climbed into bed the night before. She was pulling its sides down to cover herself because his clothes were not much bigger than her own. She could hear Sean in their room as he got up and shuffled across the floorboards to the bathroom. She heard the water run. Normally she tiptoed quickly back to her own room in the mornings, because Brian liked to sleep with his door open at the end of the hall. But he had left for Marshall the day before to spend two overnights with the swim team, to practice twice a day before their final summer meet. Ruby lingered in the hall with Sean's shirt half covering her and relished the sensation that for the first time in their few weeks together, she could be with Sean without tiptoeing, checking over her shoulder, keeping an eye on the time. She let go of the edges of the undershirt, and they rose up to her hips. She ran her hands around the sides of her thighs and felt her skin, still warm from bed.

In the past few weeks, there had been too much sneaking around. At Bar 4, at the corral, anywhere there were other people in view, Sean and Ruby had been maneuvering around each other as if they were hardly acquaintances. But as soon as they were together alone, they changed from strangers to partners as smoothly as ice to water under a desert sun. They had been disappearing from public conveniently—and always separately—to a truck, or to room 27, or to bed if it was late enough or Brian wasn't home. It was like being teenagers all over again, but without the excuse that they were too young to know any better. Ruby couldn't imagine that the rest of Whitticker was blind to what was going on by now, but it was easier not to consider what would happen if they knew. Instead, she kept standing up tall, flashing her smile as she always had, and Sean, too, played his part of the act with his customary swagger.

When they did it well, Ruby thought, they looked to be more in competition than in love. Not that either of them was talking about being in love, though, because they were more careful than that. They would arrive at Bar 4 separately and sweep through the room with their eyes on everyone except each other, buying drinks and trading news, always with a secret, keen awareness of exactly where the other was. They circled each other as if at opposite ends of an axis that attached them at a distance but held them always apart. If Sean talked with a woman in the corner of Bar 4, Ruby put her arm around the man nearest to her. If Sean had a crowd of girls with him at the pool table, Ruby moved to the center of a circle of men, flashing her smile and talking loud.

Sometimes it seemed to her that their behavior would be suspicious if it weren't so true to character. When she distanced herself from her own actions, she could see how she and Sean filled Bar 4 almost beyond its capacity to contain them. She could see Sean's wide shoulders above everyone else's, his head bowed when he talked to women so much smaller than he. Those times when she saw herself and Sean claiming the same space with their size, their attitude, their game, Ruby understood why somehow, fundamentally, what they were doing behind closed doors did make sense. At those moments she thought, *Who would ever know?*

Only once had she felt pretty sure that someone did know. It was the morning after Carl had called, after Brian had scrambled onto her bed and blurted out the news: Carl was doing his best to come home soon. Brian had fallen asleep waiting for her and Sean to come home the night before, and he was disappointed not to have woken up early enough to tell them both at once. Sean had already left for the corral.

Ruby took Brian by the shoulders as soon as he told her and tried to calm him down. He was on his knees, bouncing on her bed.

"Brian," she said to him, "your daddy couldn't figure his way out of jail if the walls were made of beer cans and chicken wire. Now, I don't want you to get any thoughts in your head about his coming home, 'cause no matter if he says he's trying, he can't come right now." She was addressing herself as well, calming her own jittery nerves. "It isn't fair for him to tell you any different, Bri. So put that out of your head."

Brian jumped off her bed and hurried out of the room, racing away from her words.

Ruby watched him go and wondered if there was any way he could be mistaken. She hardly remembered getting up then, dressing, leaving the house. She had no idea where she was going, only that she needed to distance herself from the prospect of Carl coming home. After she dropped Brian at a friend's house, she headed for town. She couldn't believe that Carl had actually phoned the night before. He had wanted to talk to her; he had talked to their son. He had committed armed robbery; there was no way he could come home. She parked her car and marched down Main Street making eye contact with no one. She didn't want company, but she had an unsettling feeling that she couldn't be alone. Striding by the Early Bird, she decided a cup of coffee might serve both purposes well enough to calm her down, so she stopped and reversed toward the door.

Mitch Blackstone was coming out as she was going in. They both stepped back out to the sidewalk, and Ruby reluctantly met his eyes.

"Hey, Mitch," she said, swerving around him. He put out his boot and stopped her.

"Is that all I get on such a beautiful morning?" He gestured with one hand toward the clearing sky.

"Sorry," she said, unfocused. "I'm still after my first cup of coffee." She tilted her head toward the door.

"I hear you," he said, patting one hand on his belly. He grinned a stained-tooth smile that showed it was a habit he understood.

She angled toward the door again.

"Sean does a little better with his first cup in him, too," he said, taking her by surprise. "But if you're looking for him in there, you're too late. He just left."

"He just left?" she echoed eagerly, peering through the diner window anyway.

She hadn't been looking for him in the first place, at least not consciously. But hearing that he'd been there, hearing his name and how he liked to have his coffee, too, Ruby lowered her guard. In a split second while Mitch stood watching her, she thought how perfect it would be to step into the diner and find Sean there, to have his hand on her knee under the table while she sat and sipped her coffee, how things might start to feel okay again. It took her by surprise, how relieved she was to hear his name. She couldn't have articulated why it made her so comfortable, but on her face anybody could have read that it was because his was the name of the only man who'd ever made her wonder how she would do, getting up on her own two feet, pulling on her own tall boots, without him.

Ruby realized too late what she had done. She cleared the smile from her face, but remained in front of Mitch so exposed that she felt naked. She couldn't bring herself to meet his eyes, to see him look at her a little funny. She pushed her way past him into the Early Bird, saying as she went, though she knew it didn't really make sense, "Better late than never."

Ruby was standing in the hall wearing Sean's undershirt replaying that encounter when he came out of their room and sneaked up behind her. He slipped an arm around her waist and under her shirt.

"You haven't made it very far," he said with his chin on her shoulder, his hand cupping her breast. "Aren't we going?" Sean was dressed in blue jeans and a clean undershirt. His boots were already on.

"Yeah," she said, turning her cheek so that it pressed against his. "I was just thinking—"

"None of that," he said, and drew back from her, smacking her behind. "I'll be downstairs making coffee. Get going, get dressed." He pounded down the stairs and into the kitchen.

They had planned the night before to hike up to Buzzard Peak today, and from where Ruby stood she could see it out the window. The lower two-thirds of the mountain face was charred black and bare, though the flat peak itself had not been touched by fire. The firefighters in their helicopters always dumped water on the highest point of a fire first, then worked their way down, and flames had never reached the top of Buzzard Peak as a result. To either side below it, small hills showed bald patches of black, but it was the face of the mountain that had seen the worst damage. Vegetation had been seared away, leaving the singed face looming over the town, wasted and exposed.

Brian had found the last fire's aftermath so compelling three years ago that he had asked Ruby if they could hike up the black sides of the mountain once the flames were gone. When she had agreed, Brian had said they should make it a tradition, and now Ruby felt she was betraying her son, on this second hike, going up without him. But Sean wanted to make the climb. "We'll find some souvenir from the fire," he'd said, "and we can bring it to Brian at his meet." Ruby knew there'd be no souvenir worth carrying down the mountain, but she liked the sound of his suggestion, or at least that Sean had thought of it, so she agreed.

Turning from the window, Ruby walked to Brian's room before going to her own. She wasn't used to having him away, if only for two nights. She put her hands on either side of the doorframe and leaned her head inside. His room was always spotless, unlike hers. He kept books and comics stacked on his small desk, Matchbox cars parked in a shoe carton on his floor. Before he'd left for Marshall, he had added some new objects to his room. In the corner, opposite his bed, he'd hung a neatly folded red horse blanket over the back of his desk chair. Against the blanket, he had propped, lucky side up, a worn horseshoe he'd come across in the desert. He'd collected an old brush and a feed sack from the corral and rested them on the floor beneath the blanket. Brian was getting ready for the birth of Evelyn's foal. This corner of his room was his preparation for a new member of their family, and the sight of it made Ruby wonder if maybe a part of Brian thought of Sean as a father. Though it made her somewhat nervous, she liked the future inherent in Brian's vision, the three of them, herself and Brian and Sean, bringing home that newborn foal someday soon. And no matter where Carl might be or Sean might be going by the time it arrived, she could see that Brian, at least, would be ready for the change.

Sean was in his truck, leaning on the horn, when Ruby finally came out of the house.

"Easy," she said, pulling herself up into the truck. She pushed his knapsack onto the floor and heard full beer cans banging together as it fell. "Brian wouldn't approve," she said, sliding to the middle of the seat, room for a third person to her window side. She dug into her pocket for a rubber band and pulled her hair back into a careless ponytail. She patted at the snarls, but didn't make them go away. Sean put one arm over the seat back and turned out of their driveway in the direction of Buzzard Peak. They drove as close in to the mountain as the dirt access road would take them and parked by a dry riverbed. Then they walked half a mile through the sandy wash until they reached a trail that led toward the peak.

Partway up the path there was a jagged demarcation where the dry, brittle shrubs gave way to thin, fragile ash. Ruby had climbed the peak enough times to know where the path had been, but, even so, the ash made their steps slow and slippery. They moved carefully, listening to the delicate crackle underfoot while their boots grew black with soot. The late-morning sun climbed with them, warming their shoulders and their cheekbones and their lids as they focused their eyes down on the carpet of ash. They didn't talk much, but stopped several times with hands to their foreheads to measure how far they'd come, how much distance they'd put between themselves and Whitticker. The town fell away quickly as they became accustomed to taking steps over the unnatural surface. *It was like the moon if the moon was black,* Brian had said three years earlier. And Ruby and Sean could have believed they were that far away, as *any* distance from the main street of downtown Whitticker had, for weeks, felt that impossibly removed.

Sean looked up toward the peak, then down to his boots pushing through a layer of ash. The powder lifted away easily, and beneath its surface, the earth was hard and black. He kicked the fine flakes off the toe of his boot and into the air. As they drifted to the ground, he could hardly distinguish the particles falling against the solid black backdrop.

"There's really nothing left here," he said, impressed. "No

scrub, no roots." He was shaking his head. "Completely bare."

"Bald," Ruby said. She cupped her hand over the back of his head and rubbed his full head of hair.

"What are you saying?" Sean grinned, patting his hair into place defensively.

Ruby skimmed one boot lightly over the ash. "Like a cue ball if a cue ball was black," she said.

"It's called the eight ball," he said, teasing.

"Haven't heard of it." She wrinkled her brow, shaking her head.

As they hiked higher, above the fire line and onto solid, unharmed ground again, Sean pulled off his shirt and wore his knapsack bare-backed. Ruby stopped to wrap her ponytail into a knot at the back of her head. They both grabbed hold of rocks to pull themselves up the steepest stretch to the summit, to where the earth, between rocks, was now clear of ash, sandy and soft. From the mountain's flat top, it seemed that all of Whitticker was at their toes, all the neighboring counties an arm's length away. The land as far as they could see lacked any distinguishing features, so beige and flat and dry even the individual cacti and the occasional aluminum roof could scarcely be discerned.

"If I had a match," Ruby said, holding one hand out and making a flicking motion with her fingers. As Brian might have done, she popped an exploding sound from her lips.

Sean sat down in a patch of white sand behind them, leaning up against a smooth, flat rock. When he opened his first beer, the crack and fizz made a similar pop. He took a long sip as he patted the space next to him for Ruby to sit down. With two tilts of his head he finished the can, and one sip behind him, Ruby did the same. The air they breathed was thin and light and now slightly dizzying. It was bright noon, and they were as close to the sun as they could be. Ruby felt the sunburn rise up red and warm in her cheeks. The beer, too, was unpalatably warm, but its wetness on her parched throat was welcome. They sipped more slowly at their second cans, taking in the view from where they sat.

Ruby rested her head on Sean's shoulder, and her stomach growled. Neither of them had eaten anything before starting out, but Ruby knew from the smell in her kitchen a few hours ago, that Sean, at least, had had his coffee. She finished her beer and felt her eyes go heavy. Sean gazed lazily into the sky, leaning into her side. With barely a breeze even as high up as they were, the only sound that reached them was the faint hum of silence itself. Letting it fill her ears, Ruby was struck that she and Sean had never been more alone together. She started to acknowledge this aloud, but then held back.

When her stomach growled again a few minutes later, it took them both by surprise, and Sean bent his face down, slipping his head under her shirt, his ear to her belly.

"Did you say something to me?" he asked playfully, his unshaven cheek scratching her skin. She could feel his lips scrambling up past her belly.

"Sean, what are you doing?" She could hardly speak through her laughter as she tried to rise up away from him.

He swung his leg over her side and pinned her down. " 'Cause if you were talking to me," he kept going, "I couldn't really hear." He shook his head under her shirt. "But I think it was something like, *grrrrrrr,*" he said, blowing his lips into her skin, and she howled as she tried to sit up.

"Sean, stop!" She laughed, sprinkling the last drops of her beer onto his neck.

They tumbled backward on the soft ground, and he raised his head so that her shirt rode up with him to her shoulders. She wriggled her bare back against the warm grains of sand, and he shook his head free for air. He worked her arms out of her short sleeves, then put his hands on her hips and gently propped her up against the rock as he leaned into her on his knees. Her shirt dangled from her neck, and he pulled it off in a swift sweep of his arm, then unhooked her bra and sent it, with her shirt, to the ground beside them. Sean wrapped his hands around her rib cage and lifted her up as he shifted from his knees to his feet. He stood her on the flat rock, and with a final step, he joined her. He dropped his hands to her hips, and he and Ruby stood together with their bare chests and bellies almost touching as they fought to catch their breath. The air was hot, but light, on their skin.

"Sean?" Ruby said, smiling, brushing her sandy red hair away from her face. "What the hell was that all about?" She slapped her palms on his chest as if to shove him.

"What do you mean, what was that was all about?" He

slipped his hands from her hips to her belt buckle and pulled it loose. "If that belly of yours has got something to say, then I want to hear it." He ran his hand over her stomach to the button on her pants. He kissed the side of her mouth, slid a finger under the string of her underwear.

"No, wait. Look at us." She was eyeing his hands. "Hey," she said, slapping his chest again, "I'm serious, what if—"

"Nobody in the world can see," he said, cutting her off. He pushed her blue jeans so they dropped toward her knees. She moved her hands from his chest as if she might pull her pants back up, but stopped at his belt buckle instead.

"Doesn't it feel like *everyone* in the world can see us?" she said. She held her arms out to her sides, palms up in the air. She looked down at her bare body and thought how unfamiliar it seemed to her in all this space, in such bright light.

"No," Sean said, squeezing her hips. "I think it feels like what it is, which is that for a few hours we are way far away on top of everything, where no one can see us. We're the only ones who can see everyone, and I just want to . . ." He stopped and pressed her hips again, made a whirring sound with his lips. "And you, as for you . . ."

He paused as he ran his eyes over her body. "As for you, Rub," he repeated quietly, ducking his head to meet her eyes, "I'm the only one who can see."

Ruby's hands clamped over his belt buckle as if she didn't know what to do. Despite the sun's heat on her skin, she had goose bumps. She couldn't figure why having his eyes on her in this vast, open space would make her squirm. She had never considered how it would feel to reach this point, where nothing about her could be left to guessing.

"Yeah," she said distractedly, staring at Sean's cheek-bones, "I know." And knowing that his were the only eyes on her right then made her feel safer, but no less exposed.

"Hey," Sean said, lifting her chin so that she had to meet his eyes. "Did I say something wrong?" He cupped his hand on her cheek. "Is there something in there you want to say, Rub?"

She forced his hand away from her face, though she meant only to shake her head, no. A mountain ten times the height of Buzzard Peak couldn't put enough distance between herself and that life down there for her to say what she wanted to say.

"Because, Rub, if there's something you're thinking right this minute," Sean started, holding one hand out, not quite touching her face, "and if it's something you're not sure how to say, then I—" He faltered. The silence was a pressure in their ears. "I mean, then it's probably what I . . . what I don't know . . . that I want to—"

"I know." She cut him off, her hand in the air to stop them both from saying more. She reached for his belt buckle anxiously then, and this time loosened it with a quick, rough jerk, hesitating only long enough to say quickly, barely audibly, "Me, too."

They stepped off the rock and tugged at their boots and dropped their pants the rest of the way down. In the bright sun, on the patch of white sand, they stripped themselves completely bare. They hardly looked at each other as they moved together, though they were the only ones who could see. They didn't speak much on the way back down the mountain, either, whether or not there was anything more to say.

15

At eight-forty-five the next morning in Marshall, Brian was floating in the diving area, away from the lane lines, with the rest of the Middies in his group. With his eyes closed and the water in his ears, he could forget that there were sixteen other swimmers in the small area with him, that around them the risers were filling up with parents watching. There were less than fifteen minutes left to float, and Brian was focusing on his four races coming up. It was what Sherley Wadlow had told them to do, to use their floating time for concentration, visualization, to imagine holding blue ribbons in their hands. "Picture yourself so far ahead of everyone else," she had said, "that it looks like you're the only one in the pool." Brian had shut his eyes tight, and in his mind he saw himself in a long, long lane with no one around him, skimming the surface as if he were flying. Ripples of water fanned out behind him. He pictured winning his lap of free-style, his lap of breast, his relay lap, his double lap of back. He saw himself leaping out of the pool at the end of his race and waving a blue ribbon in his hand to Ruby in the risers. She was sitting on the very edge of her seat, waving back to him with both hands in the air. In his mind, he didn't picture who was sitting beside her. He didn't think about whether it should be Carl or Sean.

For the most part, since he'd arrived in Marshall, Brian had stopped thinking about where his dad had gone, what his mom was doing, why, exactly, Sean was living in their house. No one in Marshall knew that his father was in jail or that Brian was pretty sure his mother and his father's brother were sometimes sharing the same bed. In Marshall, when he talked with his teammates at lunch or while they played games at the house where he'd been staying, Brian could pretend these things were not happening at home at all. Instead, he could talk about his family as he wanted to remember it: His father was a head wrangler at the corral; his mother was the most beautiful woman in town. They lived in a house at the outskirts of Whitticker, where he had a dog named Max and a big bedroom and a bike. Even though he didn't really like to ride horses, pretty soon he would even have his own foal. Brian found that outside of Whitticker he actually liked to tell other kids about himself. Removed from those few dusty roads where he'd spent his whole life, he could pick out what it was about himself that he wanted to repeat. Marshall offered Brian the same escape that floating did, taking him far away from everything he never wanted to see.

But in the last few minutes before the meet began, Brian had other things to think about besides his mother and father and Sean. On his back in the water, he intended to float without touching another swimmer or bumping a wall while he ran through each of his four races one more time. He was going to visualize his outstretched arms cutting through the water, sleek and clean, and he was going to keep his thoughts of home far away. But floating in the diving area, Brian also pictured how, once he *was* back at home, he would tack his ribbons on the frame of the mirror above his bureau. He would hang them symmetrically, two on each side. And he wouldn't have to consider how to balance the ribbons' colors, because in his mind he pictured them all blue.

High up in the risers, next to Sean, Ruby was trying to figure out which swimmer was Brian. She'd hoped to arrive in time to find a seat closer to the pool, but the only ones left were in the last rows from the top. From such a distance, it was hard to make out exactly who was who. Ruby thought it was an odd sight to be staring down upon, those seventeen little bodies floating like so many pieces of driftwood in so small a space. She'd seen them floating plenty of times before at the end of practices, but never from the vantage point she had now. The swimmers appeared to her to be all exactly the same size. They were angled carefully in place, rising and falling with the cradling ripples of the water, their arms outstretched like warnings to anyone who might get close. Ruby thought it strange that even with the water bobbing and pushing them around, no two little swimmers ever seemed to bump against each other. She watched them as she might have watched a pack of sleeping animals in a zoo, waiting for the swish of a tail or the swat of a paw that would prove to her they were indeed alive. When Sherley Wadlow blew her whistle, Ruby herself relaxed to see them all snap out of it, their enlivened bodies curling and squirming as they splashed to the corner where Sherley stood. Ruby spotted Brian then in his skinny red racing suit, the first swimmer out of the pool. He was shaking his wiry legs loose one at a time, the way Sherley had taught him. Ruby poked Sean and pointed to where Brian stood.

"What's he got stuck to his feet?" Sean asked.

Ruby could see that Sean was trying to keep from laughing. "Shut up," she said, trying not to smile herself. "He's getting loose. It's what they're supposed to do." She looked down at Brian jabbing his arms away from his body as if he were trying to get rid of them. He stood slightly apart from the other swimmers, his head bowed, taking himself seriously. Ruby couldn't help smiling. "Stop it," she said when Sean grinned. "This is his final summer meet," she said, straightening her mouth, wrinkling her brow. "This is a big deal."

Ruby scanned the risers and confirmed that she did not

recognize faces in the crowd. In Marshall, she felt safe she wouldn't see anyone from Whitticker. Otherwise, she'd have insisted Sean stay home. She was struck by how incongruous the arena appeared, these risers at a swim meet dotted with cowboy hats and turquoise belt buckles and dry, cracked boots that would never know more water than a puddle after rain. If the pool had been a rodeo ring instead, the audience would have been whooping and cheering and throwing back beers. But with all this water in front of them, and with their children in bright, skimpy swimsuits, this crowd was considerably far removed from its element.

Not that Ruby wasn't out of her element herself. But for her, being far from Whitticker, out of place, was a relief. Here she could sit beside Sean publicly without needing a mountain between the two of them and other people. Here, no one knew that her husband was in jail and that the man sitting next to her, the one she was sleeping with, was her husband's brother. Ruby was so calm about bringing Sean to Marshall that when the starter gun went off officially opening the meet, she didn't hesitate to put her hand over his knee. She kept her eye on Brian by the starting blocks as she did it, and she felt Sean tense his thigh beneath her hand before he relaxed his shoulder into hers.

"Look, look. He's up!" she exclaimed when Brian took his place on a starting block. She wiggled Sean's knee back and forth under her palm. Brian was adjusting a green swim cap over his ears. He shook his arms one more time and bent into his starting position. "That's just how he's supposed to do it," Ruby said proudly, remembering all the times Brian had showed her the same stance from a chair in their kitchen. "He's gonna whip 'em," she said. "Here he goes!"

The gun went off, and Brian's body flew into the air like a spring. It was his freestyle race, the one he'd been telling her he was most sure he could win. From the start, he was easily ahead of the rest of the pack, his turbulent kicks spraying water high and white in the air. The commotion he caused made him appear strong. In the water, he didn't look like the smallest.

"He's sure got some fire in his belly, doesn't he?" Sean said, straining forward to keep Brian in view. Brian's teammates stood up off their bench and inched toward the poolside, cheering and clapping their hands. He had already passed under the colored flags at the three-quarter mark. He was almost to the finish.

"You bet," Ruby said, leaning forward, too. Her butt was up off the riser, her fists in the air.

Brian won the race by almost two seconds over the next boy and was out of the pool before the last-place swimmer finished his lap. He leapt once in the air as he always did when he couldn't contain himself, and spun two victorious fists in circles above his head. His whole body shivered, out of control. He ripped off his swim cap and shook his hair loose, then turned to the woman who'd been timing his race and glanced at her stopwatch just long enough to check his speed. But before she could pat his back, he pulled away, wheeled by the other parent-timers stationed at the end of the lanes, and hurried toward the ribbons desk in the center of the deck. He beat his arms fast and hard by his sides. His win might as well have been the tiebreaker at a statewide championship, the way he puffed out his scrawny chest with importance. The race had happened so quickly, and Brian beamed as he neared the moment he would hold a blue ribbon in his hand, exactly as he'd visualized.

"Way to go, Bri," Ruby cupped her hands and yelled down from the risers. She whooped for him as if this were a rodeo and he'd just roped a calf in record time. "That's my boy," she yelled, fists punching the air.

At the ribbons desk, Brian had to wait to have his name and race results filled in on the tag, and in the meantime the next event began. But when he finally held the blue ribbon in his hand, Brian ran to the side of the pool closest to Sean and Ruby. He held it up in the air and flexed his wispy arms to the amusement of the people in the front rows. Some of them clapped at the spectacle he made. But Ruby didn't see anything funny about him. She felt nothing but pride for her son and his giddy smile and his lanky body that looked too small for the fat, blue ribbon he held above his head. She gave him two thumbs up, and Brian jumped again—though this time he craned his neck to find something else. As she saw him squint his eyes into the crowd, Ruby understood. She elbowed Sean, urging him to stand up next to her. Brian waved his big ribbon again, and for a second the three of them stood there together as if there were nothing but their own energy between them. Brian did a spin as he turned to march back to his team. Ruby didn't think twice about putting her arm around Sean.

When they sat down again, Sean and Ruby were holding hands. Ruby was glowing as she followed Brian's rush back to his bench.

"You showed 'em," she said in a whisper.

"He's all limbs and heart," someone said. Sean turned, off guard, to face a woman sitting next to him. "Makes quite a racer," she said.

Sean hadn't made eye contact with anyone but Ruby and Brian since they'd arrived. "Well, I actually—" he started, and caught himself. "Always has," he said, changing gears. The sudden contact with an outsider unsettled him. He could feel Ruby pressing into him, ready to take control.

"He's your son, I take it," the woman said more as an assumption than a question. She was widening her eyes at Sean, encouraging his pride.

Sean looked at her blankly.

"Yes, he is," Ruby jumped in, bending forward so that Sean had to sit back on the riser. "Brian's in the Middies," she said, flatly. "He's been a natural since he started."

The woman smiled wistfully. "My daughter hasn't taken to it as quick," she explained. "But we told her to hang in through the summer." She shook her pointer finger as she spoke. "My husband hasn't taken to it much, either," she said, acknowledging that she had come alone. "It's a good father who'd spend the whole day, give a damn or not." She raised her eyes toward Sean.

Ruby frowned, trying to think how best to cut her off. "Well, Brian can't get enough," she said and pulled back from view.

"It shows," the woman said.

Ruby took a deep breath. As she faced the pool, Sean tightened his grip on her hand, and she felt her fingers slide on the moisture of his palm. She gave him two squeezes back and kept her eyes straight ahead.

By the time the meet had ended, it was after five o'clock. Once Brian showered and said his good-byes to his group, it was getting close to six. Sean and Ruby waited by their truck in the parking lot, away from other parents, for Brian to come out. The air outdoors seemed fresh to them after the humid air at the pool, though even in the late afternoon the heat hadn't much let up. "This has been the hottest August since I don't know how long," Ruby said. She gathered her hair in her hands and clamped it on top of her head.

"You're tellin' me," Sean said, pushing her lightly against his truck, one hand on her behind. He nipped her earlobe with his lips; she kept a lookout over his shoulder.

Brian appeared with his swim bag slung across his chest and his Middies long-sleeved T-shirt on, the two souvenirs each swimmer took home at the end of every season. The T-shirt was navy blue with light blue sleeves, and it had Brian's name in script on the left sleeve. He already had three other well-worn ones like it back at home.

"Here he comes, here he comes, here he comes!" Ruby

called to Brian, squeezing Sean's waist as she moved him aside. "It's the winner!" she shouted. She opened her arms wide. "Get over here!"

Brian fell into her hug and threw his arms around her neck. He loosened his grip to flash Sean two thumbs up.

"Way to go, big guy," Sean said. He put a thumb up, too.

"Yeah," Brian said when Ruby set him down. "I did it." He adjusted the strap over his chest. "Did you see me?" he asked, eyes sparkling, not waiting for an answer. "Did you see how much I won by? Sometimes it was like—" He stretched his arms out from his sides, and Ruby grabbed him by his armpits, scooped him up. Brian screamed with laughter, kicking his legs in the air.

"Easy," she said, steering Brian in through the door that Sean had opened. "You still have to breathe the whole way home."

Sean and Ruby climbed in on either side of Brian, and Sean started the truck. While Brian gave his account of his races, they turned onto the highway toward the road that led back home.

The late August sun was low on the horizon, a sure sign that summer was nearing an end, and Ruby looked out her side window to avoid the glare. A month ago, the sky wouldn't have been dark until ten o'clock. And while she was relieved to be coming to the coolness of September, she also felt a kind of letdown, as she did at the end of every summer. The heat allowed her to feel less accountable for her actions; it could have been just the leftover association of three months free from school, or something more. She'd heard it said plenty of times, and she'd said it herself: When the temperature rises in Whitticker, you can either stay and go nuts, or go and stay sane. But Ruby had stayed through enough long summers to know that whatever happened in the heat, in those few, trying months, would also, always, pass.

She watched out the window as a clump of brittle sage came free from a prickly cholla and drifted through the air. For a split second, she wondered what Carl was doing. The sun would be lowering where he was, too, though hard as she tried, she could imagine no more than that. She recalled how the hot pavement had burned her belly the day he'd run out of the store. The heat must have driven him to it, she thought. *And what if it hadn't,* she considered. She squinted even as she looked away from the sun. It felt like such a long time ago that he had gone. It seemed that if the heat never let up, then Carl would never come home. If only they could stay here suspended on the brink of a new season, hovering where the sun wouldn't set until long after dinner and the sky was finally starting to clear, it seemed she would never have to make up her mind.

"So lets see 'em, Bri," Sean said as she snapped out of it. "One, two, three, four. Pull 'em out."

Brian was unzipping his swim bag and lifting his ribbons out one at a time.

"Wow, look at that, Bri," Ruby said, clearing her throat. "Three blues and a red. Pretty damn good if you ask me."

She checked out the window to see how much further they had to go.

Brian held up the blues all at once. "Yeah," he said, not entirely enthusiastic. He cocked his head as he examined them. "It's just that in my visualization they were all blue."

"In your what?" Ruby asked, crinkling her brow.

"My visualization," he said. "It's what Sherley Wadlow tells us to do when we're floating, to picture all our races, how we're going to win."

Ruby nodded. "So that's what you were doing. With that floating," she said. "I was watching you."

"Well, that's just at meet time," Brian said, matter-of-fact. He had laid the ribbons in his lap and was smoothing them over with the flat of his hand. "Other times we do it as a game where you have to see who can float the longest. But that's not at meet time. That's just in normal practice."

Ruby was gazing out the side window again. "I get it," she said.

Nobody said anything until Sean glanced toward Ruby. "So how do you play the game?" he asked Brian.

"It's just a floating game," Brian said. He shrugged his shoulders. "It's like a test where everybody has to float on their back and see who can last the longest. And the rule is you can't hold on to anybody else or it's cheating."

"Oh, yeah?" Ruby jumped in. She'd seen Sean turn toward her, and she caught his eye. He winked. "Why's that cheating?" she asked.

"Because those are the rules," Brian said, peering up at her. The sun was lighting up half of her face.

"Those are the rules?" Sean asked, keeping it going. "Why are *those* the rules?" He was grinning.

Brian swung his head toward him. "Because that's just the way you play—"

"There must be some reason." Ruby cut him off, looking over at Sean.

Brian turned around toward her. He was growing frustrated, and they were laughing. They weren't looking at him at all.

"Because if your ship sinks in the middle of the ocean," he broke in with a loud, whiny voice, "there's not gonna be somebody there to hold you up." He pitched his voice unnaturally high, mimicking Sherley Wadlow's, but with a bite. He craned his neck upward to be better heard. "Because that's depending on somebody else," he screeched, and Sean and Ruby fell silent. "And that's against the rules."

When he saw that he had gotten their attention, Brian changed his tone and added in his normal voice, "And if you're floating in the shallow end, you're not allowed to touch the bottom. Not even with one toe." He stopped to catch his breath.

"Well, then," Ruby said, releasing the breath she'd been holding. She turned her head so far to the right side window that she could see neither Sean nor Brian. Not that either of them was looking at her. Sean was biting the insides of his cheeks, staring ahead uncomfortably. Brian kept his head bowed and fiddled with his ribbons. His whiny voice had hit them like a smack in the face and cut them all to silence.

As they turned off the exit for Whitticker, Brian held up the red ribbon for the first time. He was fidgeting, restless in the silence. "If I just hadn't done the relay," he said more to himself than to either of them, "then I'd of had all blue." He made a clicking sound in his mouth. "It's so stupid," he said. "The other guys didn't even know how to do the breaststroke. I could've done the whole race by myself and won." He kicked a foot against the dashboard. "I'm not doing a stupid relay again."

He held the red ribbon up into the sun, maybe waiting for Sean or Ruby to say something about it, but neither of them did. They didn't say anything the rest of the way home, and they didn't say anything back inside the house. Sean and Ruby both went straight into the kitchen and pulled beers loose from a six-pack in the fridge. Brian went onto the back porch to play with Max. He showed the lethargic dog his ribbons, repeated to him the stories of his day. But as he did, he kept one ear always toward the kitchen door, trying to hear if they were speaking again. He wanted to know what it was the two of them weren't talking about, which one of them would hold out the longest.

16

Sean didn't wait for the sun to come up before he got out of bed. He dressed in the bathroom so as not to wake Ruby and decided against running the water, though there was a bad taste in his mouth. He pushed the alarm clock to "Off" and slipped out the bedroom door, carrying his boots with him downstairs. His legs were wobbly with nerves, and in each uncertain step he felt that the ground beneath him was no longer a given. It was the same sensation he'd had all night while he lay stiffly on his side of the bed, unsure if he'd ever really fallen asleep. Judging by the weight of his eyelids this morning, it was more likely he'd spent the whole night waiting to get up. Five o'clock was conspicuously early to be leaving, but he needed to go outside, where the air at that hour was still fresh. He cringed as his truck's deep, gravelly cough broke into the darkness and silence. For reasons he hoped would slip out of the house with him, he didn't want Ruby to wake up.

Driving to the corral, Sean ran the previous night's events through his head. He and Ruby were standing on either side of the guest room bed, still dressed, after Brian had fallen asleep. They'd watched Brian tack his ribbons on his mirror when he'd called them in to see, and the three of them had finally started talking again, but only about the ribbons. They assured Brian that the one red ribbon didn't lessen the importance of the other three; it gave some variety to his display. They kept up the conversation about the ribbons, but at no point did Sean and Ruby talk to each other. Sean left the room while Ruby put Brian in bed, and by the time she rejoined him, she had grown quiet again. Sean was standing by his side of the bed, and he said nothing as she came in. He didn't like to be following her lead, but he decided not to speak because her evasiveness seemed to say that he shouldn't. And while he was aware of the unspoken distance that had come between them in the last few miles of their ride home, Sean was fairly well convinced that Ruby had something more specific on her mind.

From her side of the bed, she stared across to the floorboards by his feet. Sean watched to see if she might raise her eyes, but she never did. They waited like that in silence for several minutes, as if each were hoping for the other to pull the sheets back and get in. But neither of them did. Neither of them made a move even to undress.

"So," Sean said then, roughly, raking a hand through his hair. "What the hell is this?" He held both hands out in front of him as if the answer had taken on a full, enigmatic form in the space between them. The anger in his voice surprised him. "I mean, how long is this going to last?" he asked.

Sean saw Ruby's eyelids drop as if she had gone lifeless right in front of him. She drew in a breath to speak, but remained silent.

"Ruby—" Sean started, exasperated.

"Maybe it isn't supposed to," she said, cutting him short. She said it low and quick as she tensed her shoulders, bracing herself for the impact of her words.

At first Sean thought she didn't understand his question, but then he realized they were talking about two entirely different things. Ruby wasn't thinking about how long the two of them would go without speaking. Sean wasn't thinking that what they were doing together might have to end. As her meaning came clear in his mind, he turned his back and clapped his hands to his forehead.

"Wow," he said. It was hardly more audible than a breath. He felt a heaviness come over him as if the blood were thickening and slowing in his veins. Mechanically, he pulled at his boots, his jeans, his shirt, and left them in a heap on the floor like shed skin. He crawled into bed without looking at her and turned his back to where she stood.

"I don't know—" she whispered, but stopped as if she didn't have the energy. Sean wasn't listening, anyway. He was aware of only the slightest dip when she slid rigidly into bed, and as she pulled the sheet toward her, he shut his eyes against the thought of when he might feel any more of her again.

The corral was empty when Sean drove up at quarter past five. The horses wouldn't be run in from the upper pasture for another hour. He left his truck and walked over to the fence. He climbed up on the top rail and dangled his legs into the corral. It was the first time he'd been there when no one else was around, and he realized that the corral had come to feel like a place to which he had some claim. The deep, wooden water troughs, the dark, flimsy office, the training ring—Sean surveyed his surroundings, deserted but set, like a stage before showtime, and he knew every line that would be spoken as soon as the curtain went up. It was too dark for his eyes to see the entire corral, but in the gray light Sean could bring into focus all that had transpired there in the past few weeks. He recalled the first morning, when he had parked at the far corner with his duffel next to him. It seemed like much more than a month ago that he'd met the other wranglers, that they'd slapped him on the back. Walking right by Brian and not knowing who he was could have been a fragment from another lifetime. And the phone call from Carl that had brought him here in the first place seemed so distant now, it hardly registered as real anymore.

But Carl's more recent call Sean was having a harder time consigning to the past. Since Ruby had told him what Carl had said to Brian, Sean had been working hard to steer the incident to the back of their minds. "Pretend your mind has a top shelf, Rub," he said as soon as she told him. "Push the whole thing up there and, no matter what, don't reach for it." And though neither of them brought up Carl's call again, it was no secret that they were preoccupied with the prospects of what could happen. Ruby, he figured as he sat in the dark alone, had just been turning it over a bit more visibly than he. When the sun came up, when a new day started, everything, he told himself, would probably be fine.

He jumped off the fence rail and pushed his own worry to that shelf in his mind. Yesterday he'd been in Marshall, so there would be plenty of work to get started on today. It would be good to concentrate on the horses. He decided to check the wranglers' office, to see if anything unusual was posted on the board where they listed duties that needed attending to each day. In the darkness, Sean's fingers fumbled against the door as he searched for the latch. He switched on the light inside and shielded his eyes against the naked bulb. Once they had adjusted, he looked up at the board. Even with giant letters scrawled across it, he squinted to make sure he was seeing correctly. In thick chalk, in booming letters, the board read "IT'S A BOY."

Sean spun around and bolted for the barn. The shaft of

light from the office followed him partway. *The one day we weren't here,* he mouthed, picking up his pace; *it couldn't be.* He unlatched the barn door and hurried to the first stall, which had been empty as long as he'd been working here. Sean could scarcely see into the stall, but he could hear a rustle in the hay. As he peered down, it wasn't the body he saw first, but two beads of light flashing against the darkness. "My God," he whispered, astonished that it had really happened. He craved the sunrise then; he wanted the other wranglers around, someone else who knew. The colt was standing, and Sean knelt down and put his arms through the fence railing. He made a clicking sound with his tongue, and the colt moved unsteadily toward him. Sean reached his fingers out and closed them gently around the newborn's shaky leg. He ran his loose grip up and down the length of it, supporting the delicate limb in his palm. The colt's bone and tendon, so vulnerably close beneath its skin, felt as fragile as anything Sean had ever known.

"Look at you," he said softly, smiling, though he couldn't see clearly himself.

He strained to look farther into the stall and was pretty sure Evelyn wasn't there. But he knew a mother was never separated from her foal. "Hey, little guy, where's your mom?" Sean asked as he stood up and peered farther to the back of the stall. "Where'd she go?" He spotted Evelyn lying against the back wall, stretched out on her side, and he climbed over the fence boards, groping his way carefully across the hay. He bent over Evelyn's head, one hand against her belly. Her breathing was shallow and slow, but at least she was breathing. She was an old horse to be having a foal, and Sean had known there could be complications. "Hey, old girl," he said to her tenderly, stroking the side of her head. "You take it easy for me."

When he climbed back over the fence, he sat down against the wall opposite their stall. The barn door was partway open, and outdoors the sun was beginning to come up. A warm light seeped in and highlighted the yellow bales of hay where Sean sat. The colt stood with its nose against the rail, eyeing him. Sean could begin to see its wiry body wobble on the uneven hay, and he felt his own nerves stir the same way. Until that moment, he had managed to forget that this was the reason he'd come to Whitticker in the first place. He'd forgotten that there was so tangible a time limit on his stay. It was no longer possible for Sean to connect this reason for coming to what had developed since he'd moved in. And though he'd never quite pictured the day the foal would be born, nevertheless he knew this was far from how he might have imagined it. Evelyn was suffering, and her colt had been alive for a day without Sean's knowing. He hadn't wanted this day to come. But now the sun was rising, and there he was, with only a few hours left before he would have to phone Ruby and Brian to let them know.

He wouldn't have guessed he could fall asleep at all right then, much less fall asleep soundly. But by the time Sean became aware of someone else in the barn, Lyle Fredericks was shaking him with both hands on his shoulders.

"This what you call a watchful eye?" he asked when Sean finally opened his.

"I, ah . . . wow," Sean said, looking around him, rubbing his hand over his face. "How long have I, ah . . . What time is—"

"It's too late for you to see something you shouldn't of missed." Lyle smacked Sean's head. He stepped away from Sean and peered in on the colt. "My Lord, it was a day," he said. He clapped his hands together. "That's all I can say about it. That little guy fought his way out here, and me and Mitch got our hands in there, and Evelyn—" He paused, pouting his lips. "Well, we'll be keeping an eye on Evelyn. She kind of looks like she had a longer day than the rest of us, but what do you expect? What I want to know is who the hell told all of you, 'cause we were going to do something, hang up a big bow or something."

"No, I just came in early," Sean said, trying to estimate what time it must be. "I woke up early and drove down to see what needed to get done, and then I saw the board. But Ruby and Brian, they, ah, they have no idea."

Lyle shifted toward the barn door. "Well, I don't know about that," he said, "but you've got a visitor. I didn't realize you were here, but he said you weren't home, so you had to be, and then I find you sitting here passed out like a bum with a bottle and nowhere to go at closing time." Lyle laughed, and Sean lost sight of him as Lyle pushed the door farther open into the bright sunlight. "Get up, my friend," he said. "Daytime's here."

Sean stood up stiffly and rolled his neck. "Who's here for me?" he asked.

"Brian's outside," Lyle said, and disappeared around the side of the open door. Sean started brushing hay off his backside. "Whoa, sorry little man," he heard Lyle say. "Didn't know you were right there."

Brian appeared in the wide stable doorway before Sean had a chance to think of what he should do next. If one red ribbon had caused Brian so much anxiety the day before, Sean feared how he might react to this. He walked closer to the door as if it would keep Brian from entering.

"Well, good morning to you," he said, rubbing his hands together as if he were preparing for something. He saw that Brian was wearing his Middies T-shirt again. "Why on earth are you out of bed so early after your big day?" he asked. "Don't you deserve to sleep till lunch and have ice cream for breakfast or something like that? I mean, Bri, that was something yesterday—"

"I haven't seen Evelyn in three days." Brian cut him off and stepped into the barn. "And the sun shines right onto my bed, so I can't sleep." He was looking around the barn, not at Sean. "I had to come see."

Sean rubbed his head and wished he'd thought ahead that of course this could happen. "Did you ride your bike here?" he said, struggling.

"Where is she?" Brian wasn't going to give him any leeway. He swerved around Sean to see if Evelyn was somewhere behind him.

Sean watched Brian shuffle through the hay. "Hey, actually, Bri, guess what?" Sean offered lightly, but it was already too late. Brian had come upon the colt's bright eyes peeking through the rails, and he stopped stiffly alongside the stall.

"Yeah, so," Sean started again, moving forward. He put his arms out toward Brian in explanation. "Can you believe what this big girl snuck by us while we were gone? I sure as hell can't believe it. I mean, I got here this morning, Bri, and you should of seen me. I thought, of all the days for her to go and—"

"What happened?" Brian whirled around to Sean with his jaw hanging in disbelief. His voice was strained and high as if he were about to cry. His eyebrows tensed furiously, and he gaped at Sean with accusatory eyes. "How come you didn't tell me this was going to happen?" he screeched. "You didn't even tell me this was going to happen. Why didn't you tell me?" His lower lip turned down and tears began streaking his face. "You never even said," he tried again.

"It just happened yesterday, Bri," Sean started, "while we were all away. I didn't know until right now either. Nobody could of known. And I'm so sorry we were all away, Bri, because I know you wanted to be here to see it just like—"

"Shut up," Brian wailed.

Sean's mouth fell open, too, he was so startled to hear Brian talk to him that way.

"You didn't—" Brian tried again, but he couldn't think what the end of it should be. "I don't even see where Evelyn is," he shouted. "Nobody told me anything." His shoulders rose up and down with sobs, his arms hanging limp at his sides.

Sean knew he should put his arms around him, but he couldn't ignore that he, too, was angry. It wasn't his fault that Brian had missed the birth. It wasn't his fault that Brian's final summer meet had become the colt's birthday, too. Brian wasn't his responsibility, anyway, he argued to himself. So the colt was one day old before they even knew it was alive. So this wasn't how either of them had pictured the birth happening. The last thing he needed was something else uncomfortable to turn over in his mind.

"Listen, Bri"—he tried again, but this time with less patience—"it's really not such a big deal."

Brian jammed his toe into a bale of hay and didn't say anything.

"Are you going to listen to me, Brian?" It was a sharper voice than Sean had ever used with him before. Still, he got no response. "You know, I'm sorry this hasn't worked out the way we all wanted it to, but it hasn't, and when I'm talking, you—"

"Is something wrong here?" A voice cut through him from behind. Sean felt the back of his neck turn prickly. He wheeled around and saw Ruby watching from the doorway. She stood with her feet wide apart, hands on her hips.

"What the—?" he started.

"I wake up at a quarter to seven and nobody's home?" she snapped, entering the barn. Her eyes came into Sean's view, sharp and angry. "I look all around the house wondering where the hell you two have disappeared to, and you've snuck out like there's some big secret? Is there something going on here you want to tell me about, or should I be back home in bed while my son is out here crying, and my . . . and you can't stay in bed long enough to get the sheets warm?" She didn't give Sean time to answer. "Why are you crying, Brian?"

Brian heaved and sniffled as if he were choking on his own breath. "Evelyn had the foal already and we missed it," he blurted. "We were at the meet, and we missed the whole thing. You never said, Sean never said—"

"There was nothing we could of said, Bri," Sean insisted again with frustration. "I've told you—"

"She had the foal?" Ruby jumped in. Her voice came out weaker than before, filled with surprise, not anger. She looked to Sean for an explanation.

"Yeah," Sean said, biting the inside of his cheek. "I, ah . . . Jesus, I came down here, and there . . . there she was . . . or he was. I mean—" He couldn't meet Ruby's eyes without stumbling over his words. "I mean, they're both here. Right over here. Evelyn's back there." He pointed to the far end of the stall. "And it's a he, he's right here." He bowed his head again. "Yeah."

Ruby sidled past him to the stall and looked inside. "I don't believe it," she said. She reached down and brushed the top of its head with the back of her hand. Her smile was out of place with the rest of her. Her knees were stiffly locked, her hollow eyes fearful, as she turned back to Sean.

"So I was thinking I'm going to have to stay around here to keep an eye on Evelyn," Sean told her as if she were asking. "Because it's hard to say yet how she's going to come through this. It could go either way. I'll stay until . . . I mean, we'll just have to see. Time will tell." He could see Ruby wasn't going to say anything more, and he was filling space.

She nodded absently and turned her gaze on the colt. She rested an elbow on the top rail and leaned her head on her hand. Sean hesitated, but then walked over and joined her. "Look at you," he said to the colt, his voice subdued with awe. He combed his fingers across its neck. "Bri," he said over Ruby's shoulder, "have you touched him yet? Come on, c'mere."

Brian gave one dramatic sigh before walking reluctantly to Ruby's side. He sniffled loudly as he slid his hand through the rail. The three of them stood there looking down at the colt while the sun sliced through them from behind. At the far, dark end of the stall, Evelyn lay on her side away from the sun, her slow breaths slipping from her soundlessly. Not that she needed to impart any noise at all to make Sean and Ruby and Brian aware that not everything was all right. They had known since Sean's arrival, since the beginning, that something could go wrong; they didn't need to know exactly what it was to feel the lonely ache of trouble creeping through them in the early morning air.

Carl wasn't going to hang up until he got an answer, so Ruby's phone had been ringing for several minutes by the time she returned home. From the driveway, she could hear the loud, insistent rings, and when she marched through the door, she picked up the receiver and slammed it right back down. If Sean wanted to talk about the colt, or what happened last night, or what might happen next, he could wait until he got home. She wasn't ready yet. If he wanted to know why she walked out of the barn without saying another word to him and Brian, she didn't want to talk about it. She wanted to be alone. And if anyone else was trying to bother her this early in the morning, she wasn't in any shape to deal with them, either. When the phone started ringing again before she'd even made it across the room, she grabbed the receiver only to give a piece of her mind to whoever hadn't gotten the message the first time around.

"Hello?" she barked, raising her eyebrows impatiently, waiting for an explanation. She could hear someone breathing on the other end. "Hello?" she said again. "Listen, I don't play games at eight o'clock in the morning, so speak your mind or I'm gonna—"

"That's my girl." A voice came through the receiver like a sigh of relief. It was low but sure, and Ruby knew it all too well. "Mornin', Rub."

Immediately Ruby turned light-headed and dropped to a squatting position with one hand flat on the floor. She bowed her head between her knees to keep at least some of the blood from falling to her toes.

"Rub?" The voice came again, louder this time. "Hey, I'm not playing any games here, either. Say something, Rub. It's me."

Ruby sat back and clamped her free hand over her mouth. "I, ah," she mumbled through her fingers. "No, no, I know it's you. My God, Carl, of course I know it's you. I'm just . . . Jesus, where, how are you?" She ran her tongue along the top of her mouth, searching for saliva.

"I'm pretty fantastic," he announced, his voice too lively for the morning. "I mean, I sure as hell haven't been for the past few weeks—"

"Yeah, Brian told us . . . told me that you called. I'm . . . um . . . I'm sorry I wasn't—"

"Forget it," he said. "The point is I told Brian the truth. I told him I was doing my best to—"

"Yeah, he said that you might—"

"Well, I'm coming home." Carl cut her off, and his words tore through her.

Ruby's throat went dry, and she lowered the receiver against her neck like a knife. She held her forehead and squeezed closed her eyes. *This day,* she said to herself, and slid her hand down over her face.

"What?" Carl asked.

She wasn't sure she'd said anything out loud. "What?" she said back, trying to shake her head clear. "Wait . . . that's ah . . . How did you manage that, Carl?" She could hardly hear her own voice.

"I just learned the law, Rub. Did what I had to do and beat 'em at their own game." He spoke as if it were the simplest thing, as if he'd single-handedly taken charge. "But I can tell you all about it at lunchtime tomorrow," he said. "Now, how the fuck does that sound? Lunchtime to-fucking-morrow. Music to my ears. We can talk about everything then."

"Tomorrow?" Ruby's stomach lurched. Times and dates were far too concrete for her to grasp right then. She couldn't figure specifically that lunchtime tomorrow was twenty-eight hours away. "Are you being serious?" she asked.

"Six A.M. they turn me loose," he confirmed. "Six-thirty-four I get on a bus. I've got the schedule memorized, believe you me. And listen, Rub, I know we've got a lot to talk about, and now's not the time 'cause I only get a few minutes, but I just want to say that I know you must not be sure what to think right now. But I want to tell you that a lot has changed for me since all this happened. I want you to know that I don't expect everything to be like it was right away, but I think things are gonna be—"

"We should talk about this later." Ruby cut him off, closing her eyes. "I should really be—" she started, though she could think of nothing in the world she should do.

"I've gotta go, too," he said. "I'm gonna give the boys a call down at the corral, give them a little warning." He started laughing.

Ruby felt a rush of panic. "Hey, wait, don't bother doing that," she protested. She had a flash of Sean picking up the phone. "Don't be silly. I can do that much for you, Carl. Really, let me do something. Don't worry about it."

Carl laughed again. "Are you kidding?" he said. "You couldn't give me a million dollars to let you make that call. I've been waiting for this every minute I've been in here. I only wish I could see the look on Mitch and Lyle's faces when they hear I wiggled my way out of this one. Goddamn, can you believe this?"

Ruby shook her head and rolled her tongue behind her teeth. "You know, I really can't," she said. Her head was pounding with the thought of it.

"It all worked out, Rub. I knew it would, and I think it's been for the best. It's hard to say that, but I really do."

She scarcely heard him anymore. She was fixed on one of Sean's flannel shirts casually draped over the back of a chair across the room. "That's good, then," she said distantly.

"Yeah," he agreed, and paused. "Hey, Rub, you know I've missed you."

She nodded without answering, wondering if outside of the mess she'd created with Sean, she might have missed him, too. She couldn't think that clearly. "Well, I guess that's behind you, too," she murmured.

" 'Cause I'll see you tomorrow," he said.

"Yeah," she finished, her throat constricted as if she might be sick. "I'll see you."

Carl hung up the phone, and Ruby sat on the kitchen floor with the receiver still in her hand. She was waiting for something to happen, too stunned to make any decision herself. All she knew for sure was that somewhere in the northeast corner of Arizona, Carl was phoning the corral. A short way down the road from her, one of the wranglers—Lyle or Mitch or Sean—was answering the ring that very second. One of them was shouting with surprise, waving over the other two. A few seconds longer, and Carl's homecoming wouldn't be any kind of secret anymore.

Ruby climbed the stairs listlessly up to her bedroom and pulled the pale blue suitcase down from the top shelf of her closet. She placed it on her bed and backed away as if it were swelling at the seams with danger. By that time, everybody knew. She returned the suitcase to the closet, far back on the top shelf. Someone at the Early Bird must be talking about them by now. She could hear their voices sailing over the counter, over coffee, while the booths filled up around them. She sat on the bed with her hands frozen over her knees, fingers spread wide apart in the air as if gesturing for somebody, or something, to wait. The clock on her bedside table read half past eight. The day had already been too long to be only beginning. She lay down and smoothed her arms over the bedspread in an arc, finally closing her eyes. Her thoughts spun so fast she could almost believe her body was floating inches above the bed. Around and around in the hot, thick air swirled the same three dizzying truths: there was one more night; there was a choice to make; Carl was coming home.

18

From the ridge where Ruby sat in her truck, she could see the corral below her as if it were small enough to rub out under the ball of her foot. The horses, the two wranglers by the fence post, she could have blocked them from sight with the width of her thumb. But inside her head, in the heat, nothing seemed that manageable, that small. She sat with her elbows on the steering wheel, her fingers pressed hard along her temples, while the sun poured in the window and onto her lap. Her jeans clung to her like a layer of weathered skin. Low in the sky, the sun cast a shadow over the far end of the corral where Evelyn would have been standing had she been able to. But Evelyn was lying on her side in her dark stall, and even in the sharp light of a new morning, Ruby wasn't seeing everything there was to see. Her head was foggy, growing heavy, as she looked down on the horses scattered stiff and still inside the fence. The heat seemed to be holding them in position. She squinted at the limply slumped wranglers, and a drop of sweat rolled along her hairline into her ear. The wetness tickled, and she dug a finger into her ear, then swept the flat of her hand along her forehead. She took a deep breath and confirmed that neither of the wranglers down below was Sean.

As far as she could tell, he wasn't anywhere in sight. He hadn't come home the night before, and there'd been no sign of him this morning, the morning of Carl's release. Ruby hadn't seen Sean since she'd left him standing in the barn with Brian only minutes before she'd answered her phone and heard Carl's voice. She wondered if Sean had picked up when Carl called the corral, if Sean, too, had heard Carl's voice. Had he smiled at the news, maybe shaken hands with the other wranglers because his big brother had wormed his way free? Or had he stormed away from Lyle and Mitch and the rest of them, revealing his secret—or at least a hint of something suspicious—in the clouds of dust he kicked up in his wake? In either case, Sean hadn't come home, and Ruby had a pretty strong idea of where he'd been.

She stared at the closed door of the wranglers' office. It was a flimsy door she could open with a kick, and she had rarely seen it shut. Her breaths came unevenly as she realized that all of her troubles were contained now in the small, dusty space behind it. However unforgivable her mistakes of the last month, she could wipe them out with a knock on that door. It would take no more than five minutes to walk down there, and yet Ruby remained motionless, fearful that knocking might be the biggest mistake of all. She wasn't convinced her behavior with Sean had been a mistake. Maybe not *all right,* she conceded, but maybe not a mistake. She stared at the door until black spots began to flash before her eyes. In her truck, in the heat, all she knew for sure was that *right there, right behind that door, there he is.*

The pale blue suitcase next to her had grown hot to the touch from the bright morning sun. The glint on its shiny metal handle caught Ruby's eye. It prompted her to untie the orange scarf from her belt loops and wrap it around the handle, to keep her from burning her hand when she carried the suitcase down the hill. *If* she carried the suitcase down the hill. Right now, she could hardly even look at its eggshell blue. During the night, she had moved the suitcase from the top of the closet to the bed four times before she'd finally started packing. Then she'd hidden it, packed, in the broken freezer in the basement so she wouldn't have to look at it, so Sean wouldn't see it if he did come home. But he never had. Ruby had lain on her bed, clothed, working through each step she would take leading up to this moment. But every time she pictured herself grasping the handle and pulling the suitcase from the truck, her mind shut down and she went to the kitchen for another beer. After the first few bottles, she didn't bother going back to bed. She sat on the kitchen floor with her cheek against the refrigerator's cool surface and tried playing the scenario over again. But never did she visualize beyond sitting at the top of the ridge, listening to her truck's engine hiss and click into the silence, cooling down, after she turned it off.

When the beer had run out, she'd started drinking warm whiskey from the bottle until it no longer concerned her that Sean wasn't coming home. She'd carried the bottle to her bedside and held it above the lamp, musing that with a few more slugs, the golden liquid would be gone. Not that the bottle had been near full when she'd started drinking, she'd assured herself, and then gagged at the thought that she was probably swigging from the last bottle Carl opened before he'd left. She'd spat the final mouthful back into the glass neck as she lunged across her room to the open window. She punched the screen out of its frame and thrust her head far into the night. She had thought she might be sick.

The night air had been cool and soothing on her face, and even in the dark, drunk as she was, she had seen everything with an unexpected clarity. She saw her truck, her driveway, the road that led to town. She saw Buzzard Mountain in the distance and the rigid, scattered outlines of cacti standing like skeletons closer by. In the iridescent light, she saw her surroundings cast in pearlized gray. She held her arms out into the night and saw her skin turn ashen like stone, like a statue, as if she were being petrified before her own eyes, rooted to a place that would never change. The truck, the road, the peak—they were fixed components of her life, of the person who, for twenty-five years, she had always been. Whatever variables daylight might bring, she found a solid place for herself in that quiet, gray light, among those familiar things. She felt a sadness then that she couldn't account for, unsure, as she looked out at the land she'd known her whole life, if this view was all she had left—or all she was about to leave behind.

From the top of the ridge, Ruby doubted that she had an answer even now. Except for the faint draft, she wouldn't have realized she had cracked open the truck's door. Her mind and body didn't seem to be operating as one. She was hardly aware of wrapping her fingers around the handle to pull the suitcase out the door. She didn't feel her feet hit the ground. The most she perceived was the heavy air moving past her as she cut down the ridge, along a path that would bring her out behind the office. The suitcase tugged at her fingers like a nagging child. The dry sand crumbled under her feet, so that the ground never felt solid beneath her. She kept her eyes on the wranglers by the fence; their eyes stayed on the ground. She was getting closer too quickly, so she stopped to catch her breath. The wranglers' office couldn't have been more than fifty feet away. Its walls weren't more than a few inches thick. A few feet, a few inches: it was the closest she had come to being so distant from Sean.

The whiskey in his mouth hardly burned anymore, he had sucked so much of it, warm and straight, down his throat.

On the other side of the wall from Ruby, Sean sat on the couch with the open flask between his legs. His haphazardly packed knapsack lay on the floor beside him. He had kicked apart feed sacks and thrown down tools in the barn earlier in the morning. He had turned the office upside down after that. The dirt under his fingernails, the dust and sweat smeared dark across his undershirt, were the only tangible evidence that he had indeed made this mess. Otherwise, he'd been in too blind a rage to acknowledge logically what was happening.

Like Ruby, Sean hadn't slept much the night before. He'd sat in his truck with his hand moving back and forth to the ignition. Once, he turned the engine over, but when its roar had challenged him to take *some* action, to think of *somewhere* to go, he'd switched it off right away. He had no idea where he would go. He stomped his feet on the floorboard, disgusted with his immobility. He wanted more than anything else to see Ruby; he couldn't bear the feeling that he was leaving this decision in her hands. Sean pictured Ruby at home, maybe even in their bed, mulling over whether she would have him stay or make him go once Carl returned. He tried to pinpoint when their future had even become a question to him. Two weeks earlier, it certainly hadn't been. And now that the question was out there, he couldn't believe he was doing nothing but waiting for an answer as passively as if he'd been cut from stone.

Looking into the same gray light that Ruby saw from her bedroom window, Sean remembered how she'd kept him from finishing his sentence that day on Buzzard Peak. He tried to recall what he'd been ready to say by then; only in retrospect did it strike him as significant that she hadn't allowed him to tell her. He remembered how she'd prevented either of them from speaking on their drive home from Brian's meet, how much they had avoided saying at all. Except for the brief, angry exchange before she ran out of the barn yesterday, they hadn't said anything more. And ringing in his head now was the one comment she'd made before they'd slept side by side for the last time. Where it came from, what it really meant, these things didn't matter anymore. With less than an hour to go before sunrise, Sean replayed in his head her voice reaching across their bed with words he never wanted to hear again: whatever this feels like, however it seems, *maybe it isn't supposed to.* Sean clapped his hands over his face and drew his fingers down over his eyes, his cheeks, his chin. His was the face of a coward, he thought, and he was itching with discomfort in its skin.

He found the flask of whiskey shortly after sunrise. In his rush from the barn to the office, he hadn't noticed Lyle and Mitch by the fence post watching him. Until he remembered that they kept a flask behind the cushion of the couch, he hadn't been able to focus on anything but his rage. By the time he did remember the flask, he'd worn himself out tearing apart the feed bags in the barn—but not so completely that he couldn't upend the office's contents before calming himself with a long, slow swallow as he collapsed backwards onto the couch. He sipped until the flask was almost empty, waiting and waiting and wondering what the hell he would do. He had smashed the clock on the wall in his fury; he had no idea how much time they had left. He had no idea where Ruby was now; he didn't want to think how she might have spent the night. He leaned his head back against the cushion and looked up at the ceiling. It could have been the middle of the night, his mind was so foggy. When the pounding started, he thought for sure that it was in his head. It took a few seconds for him to realize that the pounding in his head was also pounding in her head: Ruby's fist was pounding on the flimsy wooden door.

The door swung open before Sean could stand up, and Ruby filled its frame, her fist in the air. She carried the low sun in on her hips. Sean could see only her strong, dark outline against the light. Inside the narrow frame, she towered above the couch where he lay slumped with his hands and legs splayed in all directions. She'd left the suitcase where he couldn't see it, outside the open door. Sean couldn't for the life of him pull free from the weight of the whiskey, the cushions, the heat and its pressure in the air. Ruby wasn't sure how, with him right in front of her, she could possibly begin. The two of them waited, paralyzed by the silence, like two wind-up toys run out of steam—wide-eyed, poised to move, but powerless. Ruby locked her legs so tight she began to lose balance, and the grating of her boot across the gritty floorboards as she caught herself startled them both. She shifted out of the daylight. Her eyes and her hair and the soft blue of her old jeans came instantly into Sean's view; he felt the sight of them in his stomach. Her eyes adjusted to the dark, and Sean's tired face, his filthy, twisted undershirt, came clear to her. His shirt was bunched up, so that she could see the pale hairs on his belly. She saw the flask tilting precariously against the inside of his thigh. His feet were resting on the wooden table in front of him. Ruby felt that her own feet had not yet touched the ground. And though she knew, of course, that there was a floor beneath her, a roof above her, a day happening beyond those four walls, Ruby felt suspended. When she finally spoke, even her voice seemed detached from the rest of her.

"I woke you up," she said. Her voice fell out so flat and scared she didn't want to claim it as her own. Never had she intended to sound meek, apologetic.

Sean did not respond at first. He lowered his chin to his chest and glanced down the length of his body. He exhaled twice, slow and deep. "Do I look like I've slept?" he finally said.

She looked away from him, anywhere but toward the couch. The office was a mess, and from the middle of it she saw how sour things had turned. "Do I look as bad as you?" She tried to smile, but her lips trembled.

"You didn't sleep so much, either?" he asked.

"I was waiting for you," she said.

Sean dropped his feet to the floor with a thud. "We're both waiting," he said, as if annoyed she would insinuate she had more to worry about than he. He sat up as best he could.

In truth, he was far from annoyed. "What time is it, anyway?" he asked wearily.

"Barely nine," she responded without checking her watch. Their sentences hung jaggedly between them. She looked to the smashed clock on the wall. "What did you—"

"Barely three hours." He stopped her.

She held the end of her sentence in her mouth as if it blocked her breath. Neither of them wanted time to move any faster. Neither of them said anything. Outside, one of the wranglers yelled for someone to bring a stirrup.

"Sean—" Ruby cried out with so little anger in her voice that she thought she might lose control.

Sean held the flask in his fingers. "Come on, Rub," he said quietly, gently, gesturing with two fingers for her to start it coming. He collapsed back, resigning himself. "What are you going to tell me?" he asked. "What's it gonna be?"

"What do you mean, what's it going to—" she tried and stopped. She wanted to deny what was happening, but there wasn't the time, anymore, to fool themselves. Nevertheless, she was surprised to hear Sean talk that way. It hadn't occurred to her that he might have been expecting what she had to say.

"The time, Rub," he said, tapping his wrist where his watch would have been had he not thrown it to the truck's floor during the night. It was easiest to sound callous; he could wait only so long.

"Yeah," she said, turning in slow motion to the door. She

disappeared outside, and for an instant Sean thought she might leave.

"Hey—" He sat up suddenly, fighting the fear of what it might be like if she actually did walk away from him. But she returned as quickly as she'd disappeared, and Sean relaxed back into the couch. She closed the door behind her, shutting out the light. She held the blue suitcase across her legs, both hands on the wrapped handle. She heaved it onto the table in front of him and watched his whole face change before her eyes. Every muscle from his brow to his jaw seemed to soften. He breathed a long sigh of relief. The pale blue vinyl smacked on the wood like a snap of two fingers, and with that he was entirely changed.

She couldn't shake his stare. More than anything, she wanted to get away then, but he held her eyes expectantly as if, in a minute more, there would still be something that they shared. The whole time she felt as if she were lying.

"Oh, God, Rub." He started talking fast when he finally broke his silence. He shook both fists in the air as if they were the handpainted rattles she sold at the Trading Post. He shook them with a steady rhythm, like heartbeats. "Oh, Jesus, thank God." He looked to the ceiling as if he wanted to kiss it, and Ruby fell mute at his deception. "Okay, now . . . okay, good," he kept going. "Okay, listen, listen," he spoke faster and faster, shifting his weight forward to the edge of the couch. "All right, Rub," he said, reaching out to her, "we've got to talk now, about all this, about everything—what we're gonna . . . or where we should—or maybe we should just go. I don't know." He whipped his head around to check the broken clock. "Goddamn," he said. "Rub, for a second there I really thought you might . . . Nevermind, it doesn't matter now. Now we've got to get going, right? Or what, Rub? Come on, talk, talk, talk. What's going on? Or you can tell me later. Brian's outside?" He said it as if it were an assumption. Ruby said nothing. "Rub?" he prodded, bowing his head to catch her eyes.

As if she'd been slapped, she turned her face away and bent over the suitcase, clicking it open. This was her decision. Deep inside she knew it probably had been hers all along, but only with her fingers on the metal latches could she know for sure. She raised the lid, then backed away from the table as if she expected something to explode. She angled toward the door, her back partway turned to Sean.

Inside the suitcase, his jeans were stacked in a neat pile on one side; his undershirts were piled on top of them. His kerchiefs, his silk rodeo shirts, his socks in balls, were laid carefully to the other side. His razor and his toothbrush were in the worn leather pouch on top. In the silence, Ruby could almost hear his mind taking it all in. She could feel his eyes raging even as she closed her own. The office had grown so hot she felt she was forcibly holding a space for herself in the claustrophobic air. If she could just keep from caving in for a few more minutes, she knew, then it would all be done.

Her legs buckled forward and she almost tumbled to the ground as Sean kicked the table violently into the back of her knees.

"So what the hell is this?" he shouted as she spun to face him. He slammed his hand against the suitcase. "I mean, what the *fuck* is this, Ruby?" The anger in his voice hit her harder than the table.

"I'm sorry," she whispered.

"YOU'RE SORRY." He leapt up, incredulous. He grabbed a handful of his kerchiefs and socks and undershirts and hurled them across the room. The leather pouch came open, and the razor flew out and split in two against the far wall. "What the fuck do you mean, you're sorry, Ruby?" Sean kicked the suitcase off the table. "Is that all you have to say? My fucking God."

"Sean, please—" she begged.

"Please, what?" he said before she could finish. "What is it I can do for you now, Rub? What works best for you now?" He shook his hands in the air. "Should I get my shit back in my truck and slip out of town before noon? Is that what I can do for you now? Is that what you waited until nine A.M. to tell me? Or should I just plant myself out front and turn into a fucking pumpkin before your *husband* gets home?"

He kicked the table again, and Ruby jumped out of the way. She crossed her arms to steady herself. Her decision had already been made. It didn't matter what she wanted to say. "It's the way it has to be," she told him carefully, automatically. "You didn't really think I'd let you stay?" She had to say it. She had to make it fast and clear. It was not her own voice talking, and Sean knew it as well as she.

"Oh, I'm sorry, Rub," he said belligerently. "Has it been

that obvious?" His voice was mean with sarcasm. "Have I missed all the signs that this has been such a bad thing?"

Ruby started to open her mouth.

"No, don't give me any of the bullshit reasons you've spent all night trying to convince yourself are true. Don't give me any of your bullshit lies," he said, picking up speed, " 'cause . . . I won't be here long enough to hear them." He hesitated only slightly before grabbing his knapsack and starting toward the door. Drunk as he was, he was trying to move too fast.

"FOR GOD'S SAKE," Ruby shouted before he was close enough to reach the latch. He stopped, shocked, in mid-step, and turned to face her. It was the first time the whole morning that her voice had sounded like her own. It could have been a smack in the face, a splash of cold water across their eyes; it snapped them both back to their senses. For the first time since she'd entered the office, there was a possibility they might each put aside this desperation long enough to become the person the other already knew. "For God's sake," Ruby whispered. "He's your brother." She was entirely exhausted.

Sean dropped his knapsack. "He's my brother, he's your husband, he's a thief," he said calmly, though his voice reflected little patience. "There it is, Rub. What about it?"

"Oh, come on, Sean," she said, exasperated. "I know this isn't what we—" she faltered. "Don't act so fucking stupid. Don't treat me like—"

"He's also a drunk, a bum you wanted out of your house,

a fucking criminal who was taking off with your truck. He's a lazy shit, a lousy father—"

"He's Brian's father." She cut him off sternly, and Sean shut his mouth. He drew his head back, surprised, and studied her as if he was noticing something he hadn't seen before.

"Is that what this is about?" he asked. He narrowed his eyes as if maybe things were finally coming clear.

"Brian's eight years old," she said.

"Is that what this is about?" he asked again, confused. Ruby's eyes were darting; her foot had started tapping on the floor. She couldn't bring herself to say that, no, this didn't even have to do with Brian.

Sean banged his knuckles against each other. "Listen, Rub, the clock's ticking," he said, as if he'd had enough. "I know it's not your style, but this time you're actually going to have to do some talking, Ruby. Fast."

She winced at his words. She would rather have run out the door than try to say what she was thinking, and she hated that Sean had come to know it, too. But there was too much room for error, trying to put into words what she kept only in her head. "We've never really talked," she said.

"You've never talked." He wasn't going to give her any leeway.

She hid her cheek against her shoulder as if there were something about herself she couldn't stand to have him see. "I don't know," she said into her shirtsleeve.

"Ruby," he said, exasperated.

"What?" She prayed he would do the talking for her. There was no way they weren't thinking the same things.

"Nothing." He gave up.

She tried hard to clarify what she'd been struggling with in her mind for a month. She knew it had something to do with his being Carl's brother. She knew it had something to do with his being Brian's uncle. But she didn't know, no matter how hard she thought it out, what exactly he was to her. She had attached herself to her husband's brother, her son's uncle, but it was an attachment that she couldn't put her finger on—that she didn't *dare* to put her finger on. It had something to do with that.

"What is this, anyway?" she finally asked. It was the closest she could come to what she needed to say.

Sean scanned the room. He looked at the table, the suitcase, the blackboard—all things he couldn't see without seeing her in them as well. He looked at the door and knew that beyond it stood the horses and the wranglers, also inextricably tied to her. He shook his head in disbelief that it didn't bother him. With the heat swelling his head, Sean stood in a place that he'd known only with Ruby, and he did not want to leave.

"What?" Ruby jumped on him. "Tell me. Is this—"

"Nothing," he said defensively, as if he'd had a thought too honest for his own comfort.

Ruby sat down on the table, defeated. For weeks, she had prepared herself for him to say that. All those times she'd refrained from telling Sean what he meant to her made that word falling from his lips hit her a little more easily now. It was all done. She had attached herself to something. She couldn't put her finger on what it was, but now he'd said it, what she'd worried all along was true. He had called it nothing. She had attached herself to nothing. It was the way she once liked it; now it just seemed tiring. She didn't say another word.

Sean began to pace around the room. For lack of anything else to do, he started cleaning up the mess. He picked up his shirts one by one, piled them in his arms. He thought it must be getting late. They were getting nowhere. When he had all his clothes gathered together, he pushed them back into the suitcase. "I mean, I don't know what this is," he said abruptly when he finished. They needed to get things going.

Ruby faced him. She, too, knew it was getting late. Sean stood with the suitcase at his feet. It was too stuffy to stay inside. Ruby couldn't remember anything else she had wanted to say. This wasn't at all how she had pictured it. "I need to go," she said. She stepped to his side to get to the door.

"Oh. Well, that's terrific, Rub," Sean said, throwing up his arms, hitting her shoulder as he did. He stamped his boot on top of the suitcase. "Now you're all done, aren't you? You've given me my stuff, and you don't need to talk about it. You just need to go. You know, that's really fantastic."

"Sean, my God, if you even think that I *want* you to go—"

"No, I mean that's really upstanding of you, Ruby." He wasn't going to let her in. "I mean, here we are with these same few hours to deal with, with this same fucking fiasco to deal with," he said, "and everybody needs *something*, don't they, Rub? Brian needs his dad, and fucking Carl needs help, and pretty soon that colt out there's going to need a mother, and I—" He stopped himself short, aware that there was no end to his sentence that did not strike too raw a nerve. "I, ah—" He tried again to make his loose end less conspicuous. But he couldn't think of what to say.

What? Ruby could have sworn she said it out loud. Not that either of them needed to speak to understand what was going unsaid. They stood there in the middle of a mess with no right choices before them. They remained in silence with their eyes on each other until it was clear that on this much, at least, they agreed.

"And you need me to go," Sean finished. He dug his chin into his shoulder and clenched his jaw. Neither of them moved.

The heat in the office wound through the room like a third person between them who wouldn't let them alone. It came at them from every angle, compressing itself, the time, their silence. Thick within it was the sensation that nothing could get out. No words, no movement, no thoughts, could come clear. And time was passing. Ruby ground her boots into the floor so forcefully she could feel her heartbeat in her burning heels. Sean knew he was going to have to do something. When he reached for the suitcase, Ruby had already braced herself hard. She, too, knew that something had to give. When Sean raised the suitcase over his shoulder and started to yell, she squeezed shut her eyes. She started yelling, too, until she heard the wood splinter, the boards snap, as he hurled the suitcase through the door. She heard the blue vinyl smack on the porch outside, then tumble and thud in the dirt. She heard a wood panel creak as it swung loose from the door, then broke and fell onto the floor. She heard a splash of water hit the porch.

"What?" She said it out loud this time and opened her eyes. A new gust of hot air came into the room through the broken door, and Sean advanced toward it to investigate the source of the unexpected splash. He climbed sideways through the jagged hole in the door.

"Oh, God," she heard him say. She followed him out through the opening. In the daylight, in all that air, she lost her breath.

Brian was standing to the side of the broken door with a bucket, now empty, at his feet. His cheek beneath his left eye and part of his forehead above his eyebrow were cut and red with blood. He stared up at Sean and Ruby, stunned. If it hurt him where he had been hit, he showed no sign. If he even knew the door had broken open onto him, he didn't register it. Except for the scratches spreading red across his cheek, he looked no different than he would have on any other morning coming to take care of Evelyn. He stood wide-eyed, completely still. Only his eyes glared at them with shock; he wasn't even close to crying.

"Oh, my God," Ruby exclaimed, crouching down to Brian. She hugged him to her, holding the base of his neck as she had when he was born. "I'm sorry," she said desperately. "God, I'm sorry." Her voice flooded with apologies dated years before she'd ever known Sean. "Bri, I'm so, *so* sorry." She couldn't stop herself. For every curt word, every lash of impatience, every time she'd acted like a child instead of a mother, treated Carl like a burden instead of Brian's father, Ruby squeezed Brian to her, emptying herself of apologies for all the things she hadn't done right.

Sean had run inside the office, and he returned with a warm, wet rag and a sliver of soap. "Here," he said, handing the rag to Ruby. "It's clean." He winced as he assessed Brian's cuts, as if the stinging were his own. Then Sean, too, crouched down so that Brian stood the tallest of the three. Sean cupped one hand over Brian's shoulder, and as Ruby started to swab Brian's cuts gently, she wrapped her free hand around Brian's other twiggy arm. They would have made a complete ring there on the porch, except that Sean and Ruby did not reach out for one another. They concentrated on Brian, their hands maintaining a fragile but steady connection through him, their wiry conductor.

Ruby dabbed the cloth below Brian's eye, flinching herself when it touched his skin. "It might sting a little," she said sheepishly. "Tell me if it stings." She folded the cloth in half to hide the red stains. "I'm so sorry," she said again.

Brian didn't say a word. His head bobbed backwards with Ruby's careful pats, but his eyes remained fixed vacantly ahead.

"It doesn't look so bad, Bri," Sean offered lightly. "A few scratches, but I bet you don't even get a scar to brag about."

Sean thought Brian's lips might have curled upwards, and he looked to see if Ruby had noticed, too. He watched her dot the rag above Brian's eyebrow, her own eyes narrowed critically as if she were finishing a painting. Sean tightened his grip over Brian's shoulder, but the truth was he wanted to wrap his arms around Ruby. He did not want to let go of the tenderness of this exchange, even if it had been born in anger. He surveyed the disarray of clothes and puddles, the broken slices of wood and the suitcase wide open on its side like the gaping jawbone of a coyote skull in the desert. Though it was far from perfect, he did not want to lose this picture of the three of them together, amidst these scattered pieces, cleaning up the mess.

"Ruby," he said then, pleading. "Ruby, please rethink this." He was squeezing Brian's shoulder as if it were hers. "We can do this," he continued. "We can all go. Anywhere you want. I don't care."

Ruby kept wiping Brian's face and didn't respond to Sean.

"Come on," he insisted. "You can't pretend this isn't happening."

Ruby closed her eyes to a count of three and then resumed examining Brian's cuts, wetting a new corner of the rag with her saliva.

"But what we *can* do." Sean raised his voice. "What we can do right now is pack another couple bags and go. At least for a while, at least until we can think about this some more. So we're not making a decision right now, like this."

Sean grabbed one of his silk rodeo shirts out of a pool of water and flung it over his shoulder. "Ruby—"

"Sean, stop it," she pleaded in a high-pitched whisper.

"Would you look at me?" he demanded.

Ruby wrung the cloth in her hands.

"Look at *us?*" Sean shook Brian's shoulder hard enough that Brian took a sudden step back to keep his balance. "The three of us," he said in a hushed voice.

Sean and Ruby tightened their hold on Brian and drew him back. Ruby cast her eyes to the ground and let the rag fall from her hand.

For the first time since the door broke open, Brian snapped out of his daze and turned his head in a slow sweep around the porch, scanning the wet contents of the suitcase and the pieces of wood that had hit him. "Where are you going to?" he asked simply, not specifying to whom his question was directed. His voice came out calm and curious. Unlike Sean's and Ruby's, it was not desperate, not sorry, not on the brink of tears. In the midst of all the commotion, he only wanted to understand what was going on. "I said, where are you going to?" he repeated plainly when neither of them answered.

Ruby raised her head to Sean and squared her shoulders. Five more words and she'd be done. "I'm not going to anywhere," she said slowly, definitely, staring hard at Sean. She left no room for rebuttal.

Brian didn't seem bothered that she hadn't addressed her answer to him, only slightly doubtful that she was telling the truth. He looked at the suitcase again; he wanted to know what she wasn't telling him. "Is Sean going somewhere?" he persisted. He knew the suitcase hadn't been packed, or unpacked, by itself.

Ruby gave Sean a weak smile. "Sean's always going somewhere, Bri," she said softly.

Brian looked to Sean, but it was no use. Sean had locked his eyes on Ruby, also waiting for a better answer. Brian sighed as if, explanation or no explanation, he'd had enough of asking. "Well, I'm going to feed Evelyn," he announced, rolling his shoulders to free himself from their hold. His sudden decision broke Sean's and Ruby's gaze, and they both dropped their hands off Brian's shoulders. From where they crouched, they looked up to Brian for some sign of what they should do. They stared at his cuts because it was hard to do otherwise, and after a moment of hesitation, of evaluating if Brian was cleaned up well enough to go off on his own, both Sean and Ruby leaned forward instinctively, in time with each other, and kissed his eye. When their lips touched, it was a surprise, almost a collision, but they held themselves there, kissing each other, kissing Brian's eye. The three of them balanced precariously on the pressure of each other as all the pieces, for an instant, came together: Water on the porch. Clothes in a heap. Wooden planks in shards. Their lips on Brian's eye. Their meeting point.

"All right," Brian gasped when he couldn't keep still any longer. He pushed forward restlessly, separating Sean and Ruby. "I'm going," he said impatiently, picking up the empty bucket and heading down the porch steps in the opposite direction from Evelyn's stall, toward the water pump. "And we need to think of a name for the colt," he called out without turning around, his voice strong with responsibility, both feisty and proud that he seemed to be the only one capable of doing anything right.

Ruby stood up to watch him go. She watched his little body march away with bouncy strides, the bucket swinging at his side. He jumped off the second step at the far end of the porch and landed solidly with both feet in a puff of sand. Behind Ruby, the broken office door banged shut, and she spun around to face it. Sean wasn't visible through the gash in the door, but she knew if she peered through she would see him in the dark office, waiting for her. She could go to him right then and say, *Yes, yes let's get out of here, the three of us,* and within the hour they could be gone. She reached her hand out to the door latch and wrapped her fingers around it. They could be in her truck, gunning it to who knows where, with a few bags, a few boxes, packed in back. Brian would have enough room to take his ribbons, his carton of Matchbox cars. Ruby could pack one suitcase of clothes, one cardboard box of whatever family valuables, framed pictures, kitchen utensils she might choose. Sean could show them how to pack it up in no time. She loosened her grip on the door latch. He could plant their lives in the back of a pickup like seeds in a flowerpot and convince her that in a few months they'd have a whole tree blooming with fruit and leaves and shade to sit under. He could promise her all of that, and he'd be right. If she went to him now, she could drive down that road out of Whitticker and keep on going at the end. But Ruby was having a hard time imagining how their exit would actually come off. She let go of the latch. She was having a hard time picturing how everything would fit: twenty-five years, one box.

Ruby closed her hand into a fist as she walked away from the office to the end of the porch where Brian had jumped off. She looked to the corral. Brian had refilled his bucket with fresh water, and she saw him carrying the heavy load around the far side of the corral to the stall. Ruby watched him heave the weight in both hands, one labored step at a time, his whole body curling down toward the bucket as if the water might suck him in. Halfway to the stall, Brian put the bucket down in the sand and straightened his back. The sun was shining with its usual, merciless strength, turning the sand a blinding, hostile white around him. Brian raised his hand to his eye and touched the point where Sean and Ruby had kissed him, had kissed each other. Ruby watched as he moved his fingers in a careful circle along the cuts above and below his eye. *They must sting him,* she thought, but resisted the urge to help him because she knew he wouldn't want to be babied, to have assistance with his chore. It was Brian's job every morning to bring water to Evelyn, and he was big enough to take care of it by himself. He was the most grown-up eight-year-old around. Brian picked up the bucket again and resumed his clumsy steps toward the stall. As Ruby looked on from the other side of the corral, she was unsure if it was pride she felt for her son or perhaps a warmth closer to admiration. But whether she'd made all the right decisions or not, Ruby breathed easier now that their accumulation had brought her to this place: From the end of the porch, she could look out and see Brian in the midst of the harsh, unforgiving desert, moving forward one step at a time with his little pool of water, that small relief he had found for himself, his own way of getting by.

Ruby turned away from the office then and began walking back up the ridge to her truck. Before she reached the top, she paused to check on Brian's progress one more time. He had stopped again, a few yards outside Evelyn's stall, and he was kneeling down in the sand beside the bucket. He was touching his eye again, fingering the places where his cuts had begun to scab. Then he lowered his hands and dipped them into the water. Ruby imagined that his palms were red and sore from lugging the bucket. She imagined the water must feel sharp and clean. When Brian leaned his face over the bucket's wide rim and brought a handful of water up over his eyes, Ruby felt the splash on her own skin. It was crisp and fresh like the snap of a new bedsheet. Brian splashed several more handfuls over his eyes, cleaning his scrapes himself, and as she watched, Ruby felt the water's lingering coolness tingling her own eyelids. Even in the blinding sun, the sensation afforded her a cool, clear vision.

She shifted her gaze from Brian to the horses in the corral. They were standing with their hooves planted in the dirt as if they were stuck in position, waiting for someone to set them free. They were the horses that her husband had raised for more than half his life. Inside the fence, they stood scattered in a way that looked to be a pattern for them, and beyond the corral, Carl was on a highway, on a bus, on his way home to see them.

Ruby watched as one horse craned its neck to nip the backside of another that had inched too close, and there was a flurry of manes and tails before the two massive bodies settled again, like dust. Otherwise, the rest of them stood far enough apart that no horse could reach out to another. Ruby looked to the office and knew that from where he lay on the couch, Sean could sit up and see the horses through the hole in the door. In so much heat, it made sense that they should keep their distance. But no matter what, Ruby knew, they'd still all be run out to pasture in one tight pack by sunset, same as they were at the end of every day.

She watched as Brian shook his head to get rid of the last waterdrops on his lashes. She wondered how much longer than the rest of them he had, with his unmuddled mind, understood what they were doing. For now, they stood apart but still together. Ruby watched her son as he turned and bent down for the bucket at his side. She watched until Brian had hefted the skinny handle in both his hands and carried the water, like the weight of the sun, to the door where Evelyn and her colt were waiting.

acknowledgments

For their generous support and time, my thanks to: Sloan Harris, Greer Kessel, Natalie Kusz, Jill McCorkle, MTV and Pocket Books, my cousin John, Jack and the coffee crew at Sostanza, Kishen and the rest of 1435 Fillmore, Devon and Jessie (for decades), Pete (for good fortune, always).

And my parents.
. . . I think I hear the flowers growing.

Your mom thinks your short story is nice, your little brother wants more dinosaurs in it, your English teacher says it's the work of a sick and twisted mind. Get a real audience.

GET PUBLISHED

You have the talent. You have the story. MTV has your big break. Enter The Write Stuff: Short Story Competition and your work might end up in our new short story collection.

Don't believe us? The book you're holding is the winner of MTV's last Write Stuff contest. For complete rules of the competition, see the following page or call 1-800-454-5358 until December 1, 1998. You can also check out MTV Online (writestuff.mtv.com on the Web or AOL keyword: mtvwritestuff) for the rules to this and future MTV writing contests.

SUBMISSION REQUIREMENTS: No Purchase Necessary. | Submissions must not exceed 25 typed pages. | Submissions must be double spaced, one-sided only on 8 1/2 x 11 paper. All pages should be numbered. | Submissions must include a cover sheet with entrant's name, address, daytime telephone number, age and school/place of employment. | Submissions must be sent to: MTV Books Write Stuff: Short Story Competition, Pocket Books, 1230 Ave. of the Americas, New York, NY 10020. | All entries become the property of MTVN and will not be returned. | All finalists must execute the MTV Networks Release Form.

ELIGIBILITY: Entrants must be 16-28 years of age at time of entry. | Entrants under contract with a literary agent or with works previously published in book format or who work for a book publisher are not eligible. | Entrants must be citizens who are legal residents of the U.S. Void in Canada, Puerto Rico and wherever else prohibited by law. Employees of Viacom International Inc., MTV Networks ("MTVN"), their suppliers, affiliates, subsidiary agencies, participating retailers, and their families living in the same household are not eligible. | All entries must be original and the sole property of the entrant. | Entries must not have been previously published or have won any awards. | One entry per person. | Foreign-language manuscripts are not eligible. All submissions must be in English. | Manuscripts or submissions sent to MTV Books Write Stuff: Short Story Competition may not be submitted to other publishers while under consideration for the MTV Books Write Stuff: Short Story Competition.

DUE DATE: Competition runs from 9/1/98 to 12/1/98 | Entries must be received by 12/1/98. | MTVN is not responsible for lost, late, mutilated, illegible, or misdirected mail.

PRIZES: Grand Prizes - 10 to 15 winners will receive $500 each. MTVN will own all rights based on the winning entries and, if accepted for publication, in the full length work. The winners will be required to execute MTVN's standard publishing agreement granting to MTVN all such rights (including but not limited to world print publishing, first serial, audio and electronic rights), the option to acquire each winner's next work, and the right to edit the works. All other terms will be specified on MTVN's standard publishing agreement. Entry into this competition constitutes each winner's agreement to sign such contract as stated above. | Arrangements for the fulfillment of prizes will be made by MTVN. | MTVN's obligation to publish a work is subject to receipt of a complete manuscript that must be satisfactory to the publisher. | All federal, state, and local taxes assessed in connection with a prize are the responsibility of the winner. | If any winner is under 18 years of age, the prize will be awarded to his or her parent or legal guardian. | Winners will be notified by mail by June 1, 1999. Winners will be required to execute and return an Affidavit of Eligibility and Release, and MTVN's standard publishing agreement within 15 days of notification. If a winner does not comply with the rules and requirements of the competition or does not execute MTVN's standard publishing agreement and return the Affidavit of Eligibility and Release within such 15 days, an alternate winner will be selected. | Winner grants to MTVN the right to use his or her name, likeness and entry for any advertising, promotion, and publicity purposes without further compensation to or permission from the winner except where prohibited by law. | For names of winners (available after 6/1/99), send a stamped, self-addressed envelope to Prize Winners, MTV Books Write Stuff: Short Story Competition, Pocket Books, 13th Floor, 1230 Ave. of the Americas, NY, NY 10020. Requests must be received by January 31, 1999.

JUDGES: On 12/1/98 all eligible entries received will be judged by a panel of judges selected from MTVN and Pocket Books editorial divisions. | Entries will be judged on the basis of: writing ability (50%), originality (25%), and creativity (25%). | The decisions of the judges are final. All interpretations of the rules by MTVN are final. | The judges reserve the right not to award any prize in the event that there are no qualified entries received.